JUNEAU

Heat

Tressie
Lockwood

Juneau Heat

Copyright © February 2013, Tressie
Lockwood
Cover art designed by Mina Carter ©
February 2013
ISBN 978-1-937394-86-8

Amira Press
Charlotte, NC
www.amirapress.com

Chapter One

"Well?" Birk said, and Shiya took him in. Big, broad shoulders, and a powerful chest, tall and sexy in his jeans and jacket with hiking boots. He stood beside her table, leaning on it with both hands flat like he expected her to raise her chin and kiss those very delicious-looking lips. She stared into his eyes—dreamy blue eyes that did things to her insides and shortened her breath. His rugged jaw had been shaved clean, which she appreciated, and he smelled incredible. The entire package topped with overlong dirty-blond hair melted her to her core. This was a veterinarian? Seriously?

"Well what?" She cast him an expectant look. If he wanted a hello kiss, he better do the initiating—this time. Her belly had done flip-flops the entire flight out here from San Diego, and while it thrilled her to death to be in Juneau, Alaska, the reason she'd come did not produce calm self-assurance. She licked her lips, and he followed the movement of her tongue with such an expression of lust in his gaze, he might as well have met it with his own tongue.

A sudden urge to flee came over Shiya, but she resisted. She had something to prove to herself and to her family. Still, who the hell knew he would be this enigmatic in real life? Skype had lied to her. She almost laughed at her mental joke, and he moved to sit down.

"There you are, the little playmate I've enjoyed for the last two months."

"It's good to see you in real life, Birk." She glanced around at the pub, taking in the interesting atmosphere. Sawdust covered the floor, and deer heads hung on the wall. The light fixtures that looked like a ring of lanterns from the Old West illuminated the room just enough to see. The piano player on a raised platform belted out lively tunes and called a greeting each time someone entered the building. "This place is awesome. I'm glad you chose it."

Birk touched the tips of her fingers, and electricity rose through her hands, up her arms, and down to her nether regions. She turned her attention back to him and made the excuse of needing to push her glasses up to pull away from him. The very fact that her stupid eyes had itched to no end before she came pissed her off. She'd intended to wear contacts and look her best, but that was the first fail. A sexy dress and some slinky high heels went down the drain right after it. Early fall was supposed to still be warm in Juneau, but today had turned cold. She had opted for a gray sweater dress with a deep, loose neckline to show off the swell of her breasts, paired with thigh-high boots. Where she went wrong with the clothing and the contacts, she determined she would make up in attitude.

Shiya unzipped her jacket and pulled it off her shoulders. Birk popped up from his seat and came around to help her. The brush of his big hands over her arms sent chills chasing each other down her spine. She uncrossed her legs and recrossed them the other way while he arranged her jacket over the back of her chair.

"Would you like something to drink?" he offered when he sat.

"What do they have?"

"Whatever you want." He made it sound like he was the one organizing everything with the sweep of his hand, as if the manager would rush out to fulfill her wish if she requested something not on the menu. Were all shifters this way? Did they make women sweat to be taken?

Okay, Shiya, chill out, girl. You're here to seduce, not to jump into bed. Remember that.

When she first volunteered to take this one, her dad and her brother had looked at her like she'd lost her mind. After all, she was the researcher, the person assigned to gather available information, chase down leads over the phone, or get a name and pass on what she learned to those who were skilled for fieldwork. Shiya spent her life behind a computer screen. This was not her, but when she'd *almost* accidentally carried on a flirtation with Birk over Skype, well, she couldn't let one of her sisters take this, could she? After all, her simple job consisted of winning Birk's trust and getting him to confirm his shifter status. No more, no less.

"How about hot apple cider?" she suggested. "That seems like it will hit the spot."

Birk nodded and placed the order, along with what they called Alaskan Amber for himself. Beer, she noted, when his drink arrived. Shiya sipped hers.

"You're quiet," Birk said. "We teased each other late into the night online." He leaned toward her, and her breath caught in her throat. "Not that I'm complaining. I mean, my computer screen didn't do you justice. I knew you were beautiful, but I'm blown away by the real thing."

She lowered her lashes and toyed with her mug. "Thank you." When she looked up again, she tilted her head to the side and met his gaze with a flirtatious one of her own. "You're pretty sexy yourself."

"I do feel a bit cheated."

She touched the stark black rim of her glasses. "What do you mean?"

Birk's brows lowered, and he rubbed his chin. "I believe you promised me a kiss, and I haven't gotten one."

She chuckled. That's why he'd stood over her, saying well. "We can't have you disappointed, now can we?"

Shiya leaned forward. Even her sisters kissed their quarries. She could do no less than that. A chaste kiss, enough to entice but keep the distance between them. Just before their lips met, a cleared throat and the *thunk* of a jar landing on the table interrupted. Shiya drew away from Birk and turned to look into the weathered face of woman whose age she couldn't determine with all the wrinkles, the scraggly black hair, and the rumpled, worn clothing.

"Devil's club juice," the old woman announced, and she held up two fingers as if that meant something.

Birk said words she didn't quite catch, but the woman focused on Shiya.

"Um, thanks, but I don't need—"

"For when tired. Brew it myself." The woman tapped the bottle. She brought a pouch from her pocket and held it up. "Caribou leaf salve." She patted her chest, and Shiya wondered if the salve was meant to grow the boobs, but her breasts were a good size if she did say so herself. The old woman explained. "Heal wound from bear claw."

Shiya flinched. "I don't think I'll be mauled by a bear anytime soon, but thanks."

"Bad woman. You bad woman!"

The finger pointed in Shiya's face pissed her off. "Because I won't buy your products? I'm sorry, Nana, but I don't need it!"

"No Nana. No Nana," the old woman almost shouted.

A deep voice called something out in another language, and the old woman went silent, although her eyes snapped with resentment as she stared at Shiya. Grateful for whoever had gotten her to stop the harassment, Shiya peered past the woman and had to tilt her head way back at the man who strode up to their table. *Mercy!*

He stood at least six foot five or six, and had Birk by a good three or four inches. His midnight-black hair and dark eyes, paired with a chiseled jawline and massive build, gave off an air of danger. All that would be more than enough to make a woman either throw herself into his arms or run in the opposite direction, knowing she was in over her head. What added to this sexy Native American man was the tattoo of a knife on the right side of his muscular neck.

Shiya watched as he conversed with the old woman. While neither spoke in English, she could tell he chastised her in a firm but respectful manner. After a few minutes, the woman eyed Shiya and then spun on her booted feet and marched out of the pub in an obvious funk.

"I apologize for my grandmother," the big man said to her.

Shiya waved her hand. "It's fine. No harm done."

When Birk spoke, she realized he'd also spoken to the woman in the language the man used, but he seemed to know but a few words, and the old woman had ignored him. "Shiya, this is my friend Kotori Munro. I mentioned him a few times while we talked."

"*This* is Kotori?" For some reason, she had always pictured a small man. Birk had told her Kotori was attacked a few years back by a wolf. He had a scar on his throat, an injury that almost took his life, but instead took his voice, until his grandmother's potions healed him. Maybe she should have bought that salve and devil juice, or whatever she'd called it. Shiya took him in, blown away by how attractive he was, especially with the tattoo on Kotori's neck, which covered the scar.

"It's nice to meet you," she murmured, still intimidated by this man's size. "I've heard a lot about you."

He nodded and dragged up a chair from another table. She guessed the apology was the extent of what she would get for now.

"Shiya and I were discussing when and where we would stop playing with each other and get to what really interests us," Birk told Kotori.

"Oh were we?" Shiya shook her head at his boldness, and all her nervousness drifted away. What if she did? No one had to know. She hadn't told her dad or her siblings about talking to Birk so much online, and it wouldn't be like she were veering off from her job. She'd fast-forward it.

"She may look prim and proper, my friend, but under those cute glasses, our Shiya is a tigress waiting to get loose."

She waggled a finger at Birk. "Listen, you, you're going to get me in trouble."

"With who?" Kotori cut in.

She hesitated and then forced a smile. "With my morals."

Birk threw his head back laughing. "Your morals did not complain when I strip-danced for you on camera."

"You call that dancing?" She wrinkled her nose at him and then stuck out her tongue. "Besides, I wasn't the one doing it."

"You could be." His voice dropped low, and he reached for her fingers to hold in his warm grasp. Her heart hammered in her chest. "For me . . . and for Kotori."

Her eyes widened. She retrieved her hand and held both up. "Hold on, what? Are you kidding, Birk? We both knew we might, you know, see what happens, but we never discussed a . . . a . . ."

Man, was she being a prude now. Her sisters had juggled boyfriends countless times and dared any of the guys to complain about it. Of course, she didn't know if all were intimate relationships, but still, the girls took it in stride. Not only was Shiya venturing into territory unheard of scoping out shifters, she was being offered a ménage à trois with two of them?

These were monsters, nonhumans that would rip out a throat just as soon as look at a person. They lived by their own code, their own rules, and damn anyone who got in their way. At least, that's how she'd been raised to view them. She'd begun to question that view when she met and started talking to Birk.

"You're not for this craziness, are you?" she asked Kotori. "Sharing a woman?"

Kotori pinned her with his unreadable stare, and she couldn't figure out what went through his head. Then she shifted positions under his scrutiny, and the neckline of her dress moved to reveal more of one breast than the other. A bit of the aqua silk bra she wore peeked out, and Kotori's gaze lighted on it. The closed regard turned to desire in a heartbeat, but her reaction wasn't the same with him as with Birk. Kotori frightened her, more for his sheer size, and she got off on the fear.

"We have shared before," Kotori said.

"I don't know how to feel about that." She looked from one to the other and shook herself. "Listen, I don't know either of you well—Birk somewhat and Kotori not at all. I didn't come to Juneau to pick up men."

"You came for a mini vacation and to take pictures for your magazine," Birk recalled. "Where is your camera?"

Oh crap, she'd forgotten it in her room at the hotel. So much for the photographer cover, the excuse she'd used in the first place when she approached him on a forum for people interested in Alaska's natural beauty. Back in her room, she'd spent several minutes looking for her camera, making herself late for meeting with Birk, only to find out she'd kicked the thing under the bed. She should have stayed behind the computer, where real life did not interfere.

"I planned to come by and meet you first. Then shoot some pictures tomorrow," she lied. "The two of you will show me around, won't you?"

"It would be our pleasure," Birk quipped, and Kotori agreed.

When her cell phone buzzed, she checked the display and frowned. "Excuse me, gentlemen. I need to use the little girls' room."

They both stood, and she had to squeeze by Kotori to get out of the small area next to their table. Her ass brushed his thigh, and bolts of need shot through her core at how hard his leg was. Too bad he stretched high above her, because one could only imagine how big the goods hiding inside his pants were.

After darting into the bathroom, she waved a hand at her face, trying to cool down. When that didn't do it, she grabbed a paper towel, wet it, and patted her forehead and neck.

"Cold as heck outside, but hot as hell in here with them," she muttered to herself.

The cell phone buzzed again, and then it rang. She frowned seeing Joe's name on the display. She stabbed the connect button. "Why are you calling me, Joe?"

"I needed to know you were okay."

"No, you didn't, and you know not to call too."

He grunted. "Then answer my text."

She hung up on him.

The thing about shifters she'd learned in the basic training all of them received was that they had advanced hearing. For Joe to call, he risked the operation because Birk or Kotori might overhear their conversation and know her real reason for coming to

Juneau—or rather the official one. She still maintained wanting to meet Birk in person. Up until now, she had never met a shifter. She had talked to them on the Internet and on the phone in her information gathering, but it was her dad, her brother, her two sisters, and the men who worked for her dad who hunted the beasts and killed them.

Chapter Two

"Will she agree?" Kotori asked Birk.

Birk grinned. He reared back in his chair and stretched his arms over his head. A bit of adjustment in his pants had been necessary when he watched the beautiful Shiya rub her ass on his friend's leg. Of course, he wished it were him. He would have managed to bend his knees to spoon that sexy roundness for all its worth. Kotori didn't display his emotions, but he read the man with the ease of a twenty-odd-year friendship. Shiya turned Kotori on as much as she did Birk. If he knew women—and he did—she would give in.

"Yes, she will." He raised his beer to his mouth and downed half the contents in a few swigs. When he set it down, he wiped his lips with his thumb and forefinger. "What she doesn't know is that we're onto her. We know she's the daughter of that hunter that's been killing our kind for years."

"Why the ruse?"

Birk switched his gaze from his beer to Kotori, knowing what his friend meant. "She's playing her game because they want to be sure. Can't risk thinking of themselves as murderers if they kill humans by mistake. We are going along with it because I want to draw the others in closer, especially her father." Birk closed his hand into a fist, feeling the claws of the bear cut his palm. He blew a sharp breath through his nostrils and calmed himself. The nails went back to normal, and he watched as the skin knitted together.

"To suggest we have sex with her . . ."

Birk raised his brows. "You don't want to?"

Kotori said nothing. Birk already knew the answer to that question. His friend had a hard-on for the woman as much as he did. Birk had shared with his friend about spending hours talking to Shiya. He knew he should reel her in and back off, but there had been something about her from the start.

"She's special," he said and shut his eyes, bringing her curvy figure and sweet face to mind. The shoulder-length black hair she kept parted down the middle and bumped at the ends, the big brown eyes, and those glasses accentuated the bookworm he knew her to be, but even while he'd seen her body on the video camera, he had not grasped the scope of her luscious breasts, how small her waist was, packaged with a nice round ass he could ride, and long, sexy legs to wrap around him.

Online he had been somewhat safe. He couldn't smell the shampoo she used or the natural sweet scent of her skin compared with it. Worse, he couldn't smell her want for two months. Each night when they signed off, he'd had to beat his cock until he came, but he remained unsatisfied. When she sat across from him, all plans, all thought, left. All he could think about was how fast he could get her into bed.

Oh, she would say yes, because he would make sure of it.

When Shiya returned, Birk stood up. He made no attempt to hide his reaction to her, and her gaze shot to his crotch. Her eyebrows rose, and he saw alarm in the chocolate depths of her eyes. He breathed in her desire at the sight of his tented pants. Seeing her shift her gaze away from him and over to Kotori's pants front gave him great satisfaction as well. So, she was also open to a ménage. Good to know.

"Let me help you," he said and took her arm. He didn't even try to step back as she passed by, but he managed to resist bending his knees. That would be too obvious with so many to witness. Still, she squeezed by him, and he let his hand slide lower, from her back to her ass, and he lingered there until she dropped into her seat.

"You know you wrong, right?" She smirked at him.

"I'm not sure what you mean."

"You're not going to give me a chance to get to know you. You're going to try to seduce me right away."

He captured her hand, flipped it over, and nipped the inside of her wrist. The sharp intake of breath made him stick his tongue out to lave the soft skin. He raised his head just a little. "I would never make you do anything you don't want to do, Shiya."

Kotori stood, and Birk acknowledged his friend had come to the end of his tolerance of being inside. Kotori loved being out in the elements. His polar bear wanted free rein, and Kotori gave it to him more often than not.

"Let's take a walk," Birk offered and held out his hand to Shiya. She took it and stood. Birk helped her into her jacket and pulled her close to button it. He sensed more than felt her trembling at his nearness.

Once they were out on the street, Shiya fell into step between Birk and Kotori. He pushed his hands into his pockets and adjusted his long strides to match her shorter ones. Kotori kept pulling out ahead and having to fall back.

Birk chuckled. "When you go up to our cabin, you should wear mukluk boots."

She peered up at him, her lips pursed, and he resisted kissing them. "When?"

"Yes."

"What are mukluk boots?"

He pointed them out on a native Alaskan. The weather wasn't cold enough yet. Most still wore Sitka slippers, a rubber knee-high boot that would keep the feet dry during the wet weather. Birk explained all of this to Shiya.

"When we go to the cabin, you'll be more comfortable in the mukluk fur boots."

"The red fox ones," Kotori added. He stopped ahead of them and turned to examine Shiya's feet. "Those are not good."

Shiya stopped walking and tapped one booted foot with her hands on her hips. Birk knew by the pinched lips she wasn't pleased. "Anything else about me you don't like? Birk? Kotori?"

"I apologize. We didn't mean to offend you." Birk drew her into his arms and ran a hand over her back, but halted short of her rear. "There's nothing about you I don't like."

She blushed, and marched ahead of the two of them. Birk watched her ass in the short jacket, Kotori at his side. When Shiya whirled around, the excitement lighting her face swept him away.

"This city is so beautiful," she chirped. "I can't believe how close the mountain is, right at the end of the road. I feel like I can reach out and touch it."

"You can touch it," Kotori told her.

To Birk's surprise, his friend crossed to Shiya and took her hand. Birk dropped back a step to follow them. He thought Kotori would take her toward the mountain, but instead, they followed several streets with shops lining the walks. At a corner, they darted across to the opposite side, Shiya running along with her hair blowing across her face. On the sidewalk, Kotori waited for him, and Birk strode to her to pull the strands of hair from her face. Her eyes widened, and those plump lips parted as if in invitation. He accepted in silence, but he would collect later.

When Kotori stopped at a shop for ladies' boots, Birk shook his head. Leave it to Kotori to insist, even risking Shiya's anger, to help her see what they meant. She needed to understand the climate where she visited or suffer while she was there. Otherwise, none of them would enjoy themselves.

Shiya pretended to resign herself to shopping, although he caught the gleam in her eyes. Like many women, she enjoyed it, and Birk didn't mind indulging her. Soon, with more comfortable shoewear, she

dragged them from store to store, loading
Birk's and Kotori's arms with many bags.

"I don't remember agreeing to this," Birk
complained.

Shiya piled on another bag. Kotori cast
him a questioning glance when she turned
her back, and Birk shrugged. "We should be
used to this by now. We're not new to dating
women. I'm sure you enjoyed buying her the
boots."

Kotori huffed, "She wouldn't let me pay."

Birk laughed. "Stubborn little thing."

Both of them turned to watch her exclaim
over souvenirs of places she hadn't yet let
them take her to. When even Birk's feet cried
out for mercy, he snagged Shiya as she
passed him and jerked her to him. His cock
twitched having her in his arms, and he
spoke against the top of her head. "Enough
shopping for today. We're going to take you
to change, and then we go to dinner."

She wiggled in his hold, and Birk shut his
eyes. "Just one more and then—"

"No." Kotori spoke the word with finality,
and Birk looked up to find Shiya observing
him as if she questioned whether she wanted
to challenge his command. After a while, her
shoulders lowered, and she smiled. Birk had
never seen a more false grin, and it amused
him. The little vixen intended to draw them
in pretending to be obedient. She had no idea
who she toyed with.

Birk stood in the living room of Shiya's suite, while Kotori waited on the street. The luxury beachside inn didn't surprise him as her choice—or her family's. The room included a private entrance and private balcony. She'd gushed over the view when he arrived, telling him how she enjoyed the water, the mountains, the birds, and the whales that sometimes showed themselves. He'd seen this all his life and loved it, but what interested him tonight was the fireplace and, of course, the Jacuzzi tub. They could spend hours before one, and in the latter, pleasuring each other.

At last, she appeared in her bedroom doorway, dressed in jeans so tight she appeared to have been poured into them, and a lilac blouse that accentuated his favorite of her assets. On her feet, she wore boots she'd purchased earlier that day, but not the mukluks. The weather hadn't turned cold enough for those, but the ones she had on complemented her. They were flat, warm, and appeared waterproof.

"Beautiful as usual," he told her. "Come on. We shouldn't keep Kotori waiting. He gets grumpy when he's hungry."

"Okay, can't starve the bear."

He started at her choice of words, but she continued past him while pulling on her coat.

At the door, she tried opening it, but he shoved it closed, standing behind her. She tipped her head up to look at him, and he focused on her lips. Tonight she'd added a gloss to them, and whatever shower gel or perfume she'd used tickled his nose. She smelled good enough to eat.

"Let me get that," he said and reached around to button her coat. With deliberate movements, he allowed his cock to touch her back, and he felt the tremor when it passed through her. "That's better. You're not used to the weather here."

"Th-Thanks."

He opened the door, and they started down the short flight of stairs to the street where his SUV waited. Kotori leaned against the side of the vehicle, and when he spotted Shiya, he examined her from head to foot and nodded.

She made a sound of mock annoyance. "Glad to meet with your approval, oh great Kotori."

Birk chuckled at the scowl on Kotori's face, and they headed out. The restaurant they'd agreed on was a nice, quiet place, but driving by the port, Shiya exclaimed, "Oh, I wanted to try that place. They say you can see planes taking off right beneath you, and it's a great view of the water and the ships coming in."

Birk hesitated. "Baby, there are two cruise ships at port." He pointed with his chin. If we go there now, there's a possibility of it being crowded and having slow service. Tourists everywhere."

"I'm a tourist," she reminded him. "Okay, we can go wherever you want."

She wriggled her feet in the boots and turned them side to side. "After trusting you two to selecting my boots, I'm good."

"Well as long as you're good," he teased.

She smacked his arm.

They walked into the restaurant not too long later, and Birk kept his hand at Shiya's back as he held the door for her. Kotori followed behind them. Just as he knew it would be, the place was full, but not overcrowded. The low lighting and the music worked, in his opinion, along with great food he enjoyed. Besides that, he and Kotori were good friends with the owner.

"Birk, Kotori," came a shout from several feet away. Heads turned in their direction, and Birk stepped forward to shake Laramie's hand.

"Been a while, Laramie."

"Good to see you, Birk. You dragged this beast out of the mountains, I see," his friend commented, and they laughed together.

From the corner of his eye, Birk noticed Shiya perk up at Laramie's choice of words. Did she think they would slip and admit what they were? He intended to pull her close to him, enjoy her, and draw her family in. Then he would take them all down so they would never come to Alaska again. His people would remain safe, which was his and Kotori's number one priority. Whether the hunters' destruction would include Shiya wasn't clear yet. He'd already broken his resolve just getting involved with her.

"This is my friend from outside," Birk told his friend.

Laramie's attention locked on Shiya's chest, and Kotori grunted a warning from behind them. "Welcome, little lady. Whatever I have is yours."

Shiya tugged her hand free of his when he held it too long. "Thank you." She cast a confused glance at Birk. "What do you mean I'm from outside?"

They all chuckled again at her expense. Laramie was the one to explain. "That just means you are from outside of Alaska. There is our wonderful state of Alaska, and there is outside."

"Meaning everybody else. Gotcha." She shook her head in amusement.

Soon they were provided with a nice table in the corner, and Birk perused the menu. Shiya did as well, but Kotori always ordered the same meal, so he didn't need to look.

Birk ordered sauvignon blanc for the three of them, and put a hand on the back of

Shiya's to lean closer to her. "Have you decided?"

Her head popped up, bringing her mouth dangerously close to his. He remained where he was, watching the emotions flit across her expressive face, and then raised an eyebrow when she didn't say anything.

"Oh yeah, um, can I get the halibut on a bed of green beans, and I also want salmon chowder, please. I've never had that. I wonder if it tastes similar to clam chowder. Guess I'll find out."

Birk put in his and Shiya's order and let Kotori handle his. When Kotori's appetizer arrived before the rest of the food, Shiya watched him eat the grilled tiger prawns with cherry tomatoes. Her interest in the food was so obvious, he picked one up and fed it to her. Shiya bit into the meat and moaned as she chewed.

"Mm, that's so good. I didn't realize how hungry I was until I saw you eating." She stuck a finger to her mouth and licked a bit of sauce from it. Both Birk and Kotori caught her wrist and put her hand down. She looked from one to the other. "What?"

"Nothing, I'm glad you're enjoying it," Birk murmured.

When she was done and had cleaned her fingers on a tissue, she turned to Kotori. "Okay, so I know Birk's a vet. What about you, Kotori? What do you do?"

His friend didn't hesitate or look away from her face, which told Birk she was special for him as well. "I own several fishing vessels and supply many of the local restaurants and a few in Anchorage."

"Nice."

Birk's mind drifted while they spoke, and he sat in silence, half following the conversation. His thoughts were more consumed with Shiya and their plans for her. He and Kotori spoke the truth when they said they'd shared lovers.

A female shifter had the drive and the strength to take both him and his buddy, but this was their first time with a human. As an African-American, she was also a first, because of the low population percentage in Juneau for her race. If he had found a woman like Shiya who tempted him like she did, he would have already enjoyed her. Race meant nothing to him, but he had to admit, Shiya's smooth cocoa skin intrigued him and gave him fantasies of licking it from top to bottom. She would give in to their desires, but would she be able to handle him, let alone Kotori? Maybe it was a mistake to share her when every move she made, every sound and gesture, reminded him of how much he wanted her. Even now, he envisioned reaching across the table and ripping her blouse open so he could see her nipples. To think of holding those heavy globes in his palms hardened his dick to the point of discomfort.

"Hey!"

Birk blinked and focused on Shiya's face.

"Where were you?" She smiled at him, and he felt a stirring inside. He'd been in love once, and it turned out badly. He didn't care to repeat it, ever.

"I'm right here." He laid a hand on her thigh and slid it higher. Seeing the desire he evoked pleased him as he pushed a finger against the spot where her clit hid. He cursed the jeans for keeping him from the treasure. Shiya bit her bottom lip, and her lashes fluttered down before she forced her head up. She covered his hand and pushed it back.

"That's not playing fair."

"I don't remember agreeing to fair."

She turned to Kotori. "Don't you think he's cheating?"

"He cheats at cards too," was the rough reply.

Shiya laughed, and he frowned at his friend. "Thanks a lot, buddy."

Kotori shrugged. "I always tell the truth."

When a light of interest shone in Shiya's expression, he should have known she would pounce on Kotori's words. "Do you? Well tell me this."

Birk stiffened.

"Are you married, or do you have a girlfriend? Have you ever slept with a black woman?"

Her questions surprised Birk. Did she let the opportunity slip by on purpose? She could have asked Kotori anything, like did he believe in shape-shifters, or was he one. She could have queried him in any number of ways that would lead her closer to the affirmation that they were what she thought—polar bear shifters. Then again, this could be her tactic to make them trust her, to get careless and let her into their world. If so, she was a very clever woman, and unfortunately, the knowledge made him want her more.

"No to all three," Kotori admitted.

"Does that cancel the deal?" Birk interrupted. "That we have not been with a black woman?"

"Well there'd have to be a deal . . ." One side of her mouth turned up playfully. "But no, it doesn't. We're not talking a relationship anyway."

"How long can we keep you?"

She grinned. "I have two weeks—longer if I need it."

Something in the way she said "if I need it" made him think her family had pressured her to get it done. Didn't she do this kind of thing all the time? He wondered just how much of the personal information she shared with him was true, and what was all a part of the hunter's plan. They had no conscience when it came to getting what they wanted.

When their dinner arrived, they ate and chatted about what Shiya wanted to do the next day. Taking the tram up Roberts Mountain stood at the top of the list. He had no problem escorting her, but his and Kotori's goal included getting her into bed by the next day.

The night turned bitter cold by the time they left the restaurant. Birk yielded to Kotori when he wrapped an arm around Shiya's shoulders and drew her into his side. She moaned softly, a sound that vibrated along his nerve endings and ended in his ball sac.

"You're so warm, Kotori," she murmured from his chest, and when they climbed into the SUV, Kotori took the front seat across from him, putting Shiya on his lap. Yeah, they would have her tomorrow for sure.

At the entrance to Shiya's room, Birk decided to take things to the next level so there would be no misunderstandings. He stood above her, crowding her space. She had nowhere to go but into his arms with the door at her back. "I think it's time for me to show you what you're missing."

"You're that confident, huh? I'd heard that . . ."

He leaned down, bringing his lips within an inch of hers. The warmth of their breaths mingled, and he tilted his head a little, but waited to claim what he desired. "You'd heard what?"

She seemed to change her mind about whatever it was she'd intended to say. "I heard Alaskan men are bold."

"Hm, I can't speak for the rest. I know what I want, and I don't hesitate to take it."

"And if I said no?"

He grinned. "You won't say no."

Then he covered her mouth and explored the sweet interior. He cupped her face just beneath her ear and took the kiss deeper. Sweeping her tongue with his own, he tangled the two together and showed her what he had in store. A hand around her waist, he drew her tight to his chest until he flattened her breasts. A cry of pleasure escaped her, and only then did he raise his head and take a step back. She reached a hand to her swollen lips, her gaze unfocused, but before she could recover, Kotori moved in.

He laid his hands at her waist. "My turn." She had just enough time make a small noise of surprise when he raised her off her feet. Kotori crushed her to him, molding her body to his and giving Birk visions of the two of them taking her—one in front, the other in back. His friend ran a hand over Shiya's back until he reached her ass, and then he squeezed the round cheek until she murmured against his mouth. He forced her head back and assaulted her mouth with a hunger Birk knew Kotori fought to contain.

The grip Shiya held on Kotori's jacket sleeves went limp, and Birk touched his buddy's shoulder. Kotori kissed her moments longer and then set her on her feet. Shiya wobbled, and Kotori steadied her. "Shall I carry you inside?" he teased.

"Please, I'm fine. Good night, boys. See you in the morning."

Birk chuckled under his breath when she stumbled after opening the door and walking across the threshold. Once again, he wondered if she could take them both, but he refused to back down now. One taste had him determined to eat Shiya up.

He and Kotori returned to the SUV, and Birk threw it into first gear. "You heading home?"

"No, I'll have to visit my grandmother," Kotori said. The frown on his face told Birk he wasn't looking forward to it. Kotori might be head of his family, but his grandmother could be a handful.

"Think she knows about Shiya?"

Kotori swore. "Of course she knows. She always does. I didn't tell her anything, but I'm sure she will say the spirits told her Shiya's from a family of shifter hunters.

Damn it, sometimes I wish she was wrong once in a while. Then I could get peace."

Birk laughed. "Oh, you're not going to get peace anytime soon, my friend. She'll have you married with kids before long."

Kotori sneered at him, and Birk shook his head, amused. What would his grandmother say if she knew they would both share the hunter's daughter?

"At least she respects me as the leader— well, around others."

"Private lectures, huh?"

Kotori winced. "Enough to make my ears bleed."

They rode in silence for a while as Birk thought over the situation. "She is right, though. Shiya here means trouble. She didn't come alone. I smelled a human near her place tonight, the same scent I picked up outside the restaurant and near a couple of the shops we visited. It could be a coincidence, but I doubt it."

Kotori nodded. "The tip-off we got that the famous Keith hunters coming to Alaska was right. They always send in someone to scope out the situation, who confirms the presence of shifters. Then they move in. Backers and investments mean they can afford to do this full-time and pay off whoever they need to keep it all quiet."

Birk slammed a fist against the steering wheel. A new idea struck him. "If we capture her heart, she might betray her family."

Kotori's eyes widened. "Do we want to do that? We've never deliberately set out to make a woman fall in love. We've always made it plain it's about the sex and nothing else. Neither of us wants a mate."

"It's below the belt, I admit, but she knows her family's intentions, doesn't she? She came here knowing if she learns what we are, her father or his men will try to kill us. Should we give a shit if she gets hurt?"

Kotori stared out the front window and rubbed the scar on his neck. Birk knew he did that when he mulled over a decision that could cost him, just like the one that caused him to get the wound in the first place.

"You already have feelings for her," Birk said.

"I do," Kotori admitted. "A little, but I'm never going to mate with a human, and she will never come before family. Period."

"Okay. Let's do it."

Chapter Three

Shiya walked into her suite and shut the door. She leaned on it with her eyes shut and waited for her heart to stop pounding. Their kiss was everything she had imagined and more. In what world, what fantasy had she ever come up with that meant being involved with two men at once? Two men who knew about it and were okay with it? Her sexual experience wasn't vast. Hell, it consisted of one man, and as scared as she felt at going through with this idea, she would do it. *Maybe tomorrow night.*

She pushed off the door and bent to remove her boots. Then she carried them to her room. Sitting on her bed, she paused to touch her lips, amazed at their numbness. She didn't even know they could swell from just a kiss. Yet they had. She bent down to remove her socks and tossed them on the floor.

When Birk touched her face, she felt like he took total control of her body just from that spot. All she wanted to do was tilt her head back and let him have what he wanted. She'd basked in the sensation of his lips moving over hers, and the taste of his tongue sweeping her mouth. He held her close, but what wet her panties was the meaning in his touch, as if he laid claim and all she had to do was spread her legs. In fact, in that moment, she'd wanted him to unzip her pants, snatch them down, and just fill her full with his cock.

Where Birk's kiss and touch were possessive and made her head spin, Kotori's could be defined only as untamed. He'd been rough in lifting her off her feet, his mouth on hers unyielding yet demanding. Fear had swept her being when he dragged her closer and squeezed her ass, because it seemed like Kotori held himself in check by a thread. If he let go, the man might break her, and she was ashamed to admit that she craved his wildness. She wanted him to manhandle her. Just like with Birk, she had longed for Kotori to rip her clothes off, bend her over, and fuck her brains out.

"I must be insane," she muttered to the empty room and stood to stumble over to the full-length mirror on the wall. With flushed face and heavy breaths, she stared into her eyes. "They're not human, Shiya."

The reality of her affirmation refused to clear her clouded mind, and when someone knocked on the door, a buzz of excitement rose inside thinking it might be them come back to demand more. She grinned as she went to answer. With her hand on the knob, she sucked in a breath and schooled her expression not to appear too eager. She opened the door and froze.

"Joe."

"Hello, Shiya. Can I come in?"

She remained where she was, saying nothing. When he called earlier, she'd hung up on him and didn't answer his texts, except to write, "I'm fine." She should have known he would show up, but then her dad never told her he'd assigned Joe to watch her. Both her sisters were assigned a team to assist them on jobs, one man ordered to stay closer than the others just in case. On more than one occasion, her sisters had been saved by their protector, even though both women could kick ass themselves.

"Why are you here?"

He stepped forward, and she backpedaled a step to keep from brushing him by accident. "You're on a job, aren't you? Your first?" He said the words as if a child should get the reasoning, and she frowned at his back.

She slammed the door and put her hands on her hips. "I mean why are *you* here? I know you're not my protector."

He scanned the room as if looking for someone lurking in the shadows. She passed him and shut her bedroom door. The chastisement in his glare at her didn't mean a damn thing.

"I am your protector now. I asked your dad to put me on it when you didn't check in."

"I've been here exactly twelve hours. I haven't had time to—"

"You're supposed to check in before takeoff and after. Then again when you make contact. You did none of those."

"I spoke to my sister." Why the hell did he make her feel like a disobedient child? Then again, he'd always had that ability, and maybe she gave him the power in the past—since he had been her first. Not anymore. "Like I said, I haven't been here long, so that really didn't give you the time to find out I wasn't following procedure and to get a plane out here."

He sighed. "Shiya, the team is in Anchorage. Do you really think we'd all sit on our thumbs in San Diego waiting for you to confirm whether these men are shifters? Or do you doubt your skills? You all but confirmed with that computer thing you do before we even cleared you to take this job."

"*We* didn't clear me to take it. My dad did, and I don't want you here."

He moved closer to her, and it took everything inside to stand her ground rather than run away from him. She knew the power he used to hold over her, and she could tell herself he no longer had that ability, but testing it would not happen tonight. When he touched her cheek, she smacked his hand away. The love reflected in his gaze drove her nuts, and she gritted her teeth.

"What happened to us, Shiya? We were good together."

She rolled her eyes and crossed her arms over her chest. "Yeah, we were good, all right. Your ambition to be my dad's right-hand man got in the way."

His jaw tightened. "There's nothing wrong with ambition, and me moving up in the ranks could only help us. I make more."

"I don't need your money."

His lips thinned into a straight line, and she took in his features. Joe stood at six foot one, and his pale blond hair, coupled with green eyes, used to make her heart pound. He worked hard on his build, and she had to admit he still looked good, but she would never be the priority in his life.

At twenty, in college, she'd fallen for the man she'd thought was so sexy, so badass because he worked for her father. Ten years ago, Joe seemed larger than life, and when she found the boldness to ask him out, she'd been over the moon because he accepted. Her sister Shae, her closest sister, told her to be careful of her heart, but she hadn't listened. For a while, nothing mattered except Joe, and when he took her virginity, she gave it willingly because he already owned her heart.

Looking at his mouth now, she recalled his kisses. Joe's loving held tenderness with every touch, and because of it, she'd comforted herself with the fact that he cared about her. Loving her more than the job was the problem.

He turned and strode away from her. She wanted to tell him to get out, but some part of her desired him to stay.

"I want us to get back together," he said, and she gasped. He faced her, determination in his eyes. "That's why I'm here. I told your dad my plan, and he agreed to make me your protector. He knows I will die to keep you safe."

She bit off a screech and balled her hands into fists. "Are you serious? When are you and my dad going to get it into your heads? I run my life, not you. I make decisions about whom my lover will be, and it's not going to be you, Joe. We broke up three months ago. You should have moved on by now."

"Like you have?"

She blinked at him.

"I saw you let those things kiss you."

"It's part of the job," she bit out. "My sisters do it all the time."

"This is your first assignment. You can't afford to take chances. I think—"

"I don't give a rat's ass what you think. Get out of my room."

"Shiya."

"I mean it, Joe. Get out!" She stomped over to the door, yanked it open, and waited for him to pass by. He didn't move. "If you don't leave, I'm calling my dad right now and telling him you're here for me and not taking your job seriously."

"He knows me better than that."

"Do you want it in his head?"

He frowned. "We'll pick this conversation up again. Check in. Follow the chain of command, Shiya."

She resisted yelling "fuck you" and slammed the door behind him. After clicking the lock into place, she removed her clothing, threw on a robe, and grabbed a mini bottle of alcohol from the refrigerator. She didn't even check to see what it was before she poured it over a glass of ice. With the lights turned low, she sat in the alcove by the windows and raised the blinds so she could look out at the water. The liquid gave a satisfying burn as it slid down her throat, and after a few sips, she began to mellow out.

Was it wise to jump into bed with Birk and Kotori with so many unresolved emotional issues over Joe? She didn't know, but then again, if her heart was taken, she couldn't fall in love with them. She could leave this at sex, and why should she feel guilty either way? Any man who felt fine about sharing his woman with another did not love her. Birk made the offer. He admitted to doing it before. She was nobody special to him, and she wouldn't dare consider a serious relationship with a shifter. Enough said.

The next morning, the knock on the door revealed Kotori, and Shiya smiled up at him. "Hey, you, where's Birk?"

Kotori, smoking hot in jeans and black jacket, exuded a magnetism that drew her into his arms for a quick kiss. That she did so surprised her, but neither of them resisted the impulse. Rather than push his tongue into her mouth, though, he left it at parted lips and a brief suck on her lower one. All kinds of delicious sensations stirred in her lower region as she pulled him inside so she could get her coat.

She thought she saw a frown on Kotori's face as he breathed in, but it disappeared as fast as it surfaced. "He had an emergency surgery, but he will catch up with us later."

Shiya paused in pulling on her coat. "Aw, is the animal okay?"

He stared at her for a minute.

"Kotori?"

"He'll be fine. Birk's good at what he does."

"A regular Dr. Dolittle?" she joked and then chided herself. She had to stop making these stupid mistakes, insinuating that he could talk to animals because he was one, or they would catch on to her.

She submitted when Kotori did what Birk had done. He buttoned her coat for her and lifted the collar to be sure she would stay warm. Not wanting to think of what would come later when her job concluded, she pushed the darker thoughts aside. Kotori hadn't bothered to respond to her question.

She wondered about what he'd said the night before about always speaking the truth. Was that his method, to not answer anything he would have to lie about?

"You wanted to ride the tram?" he asked instead.

"Yes! I think it will be fun to look down on Juneau. I hear the view is breathtaking."

They left the room, and Shiya noted, instead of Birk's SUV, they rode in a Bronco. The massive tires with deep tread screamed Kotori. She had to climb to get into the passenger seat, and he shut the door behind her. When he sat behind the wheel, he turned over the engine and shifted gears.

"I noticed both of you have stick shifts. Is that just boys and their toys, or what?"

Kotori drove to the street, threw on his turn signal, and turned right. "No, most vehicles here in Juneau are stick shift. Most are four-wheel drive because of the weather in winter. You don't want to get into trouble trying to drive on snow and ice with anything less."

"That makes sense." Shiya hesitated and then reached across to put her hand on his thigh. The hard muscles contracted beneath her touch, and she chewed her bottom lip. She watched in awe as the front of his pants tented. He must be massive under there, and she couldn't wait to have him stretching her walls and plowing as deep as he could go. She would wait for Birk to be with them, though. If this fantasy happened, she'd have it all.

They arrived at the tram station and found parking. Kotori paid the admission fee, which included all-day unlimited rides. Looking up at the top, she wondered if she'd even want to ride again after one time. Her stomach stirred with butterflies, and Kotori took her hand.

"Don't worry. It's only seventeen hundred feet up."

"That is so not funny." She rolled her eyes at him, but he smiled and leaned down to kiss her.

They waited their turn to get on the tram along with a large group of other people.

Shiya found a spot at the back to look out the window, and Kotori stood behind her. He towered so high above her head, he would have no trouble seeing, and she grabbed his hand to put on her waist. He gave her a light squeeze as the tram began to climb Roberts Mountain.

Over an intercom, a woman shared interesting facts about the wildlife, the city, and the tram. Shiya half listened while focusing on how close the tops of trees appeared. When they were high enough, she marveled over the city, clinging to the shoreline as if the mountains crowded it out. The sight took her breath away.

"Across the bridge, is that still Juneau?" she asked Kotori.

"This side of the Gastineau Channel is Juneau, which includes the downtown area. On that side is West Juneau." He moved his finger left of the bridge. "Down that way is Douglas Island."

When the ride ended, they wandered along the trails, enjoying the tropical forest–type vegetation. When Shiya spotted bears some distance from where they stood, she grabbed Kotori's hand and froze.

"Bears! I didn't realize there are bears here."

Kotori hugged her. "It's okay. They have platforms where you can view them closer in a safe location, but don't worry, I will protect you. Sometimes they come down to the city. They smell the garbage. Everyone is supposed to have bear-safe lids, but things happen." He shrugged.

From his casual stance, she figured this was a standard way of life for him, and it was no big deal. She'd never seen anything bigger than a raccoon or a possum that wasn't closed off in a zoo.

"Do you not like bears?"

Her answer to his question appeared to be important to him, and she turned away. She'd forgotten for an instant what she believed him to be—a polar bear shifter. The bears she spotted were black.

"I like bears just fine," she said. They continued walking. "Kotori?"

"Yes?"

"You're Native American, aren't you?"

"I am."

"What tribe?"

"Tlingit."

Her blank stare brought a smile to his handsome face that made her forget everything but him. He traced a finger over her nose, staring into her eyes. Between them, she felt his hard-on pressed into her stomach, and she wondered if it was perpetual, or did she just turn him on all the time? The latter pleased her to think.

"I bet you thought I would say something like Cherokee?" His eyes flashed amusement.

"Please, I'm not that ignorant," she asserted and spun away. "Tell me about your people."

He didn't hesitate, which made her think he shared what was common knowledge, stuff to be found on the Internet. He would not, for example, tell her what percentage of them were shifters, and what kind of animals. For a minute, she wished they were close enough for that level of honesty, having nothing to do with her family or his.

"We call ourselves Lingit, which means 'people of the tides.'"

Shiya pounced on this information. Polar bears were animals that loved being in or near the water. The correlation interested her.

"We're traditionally hunter-gatherers, and extend mostly in Southeast Alaska and Western Canada."

"Cold areas?"

He nodded. "You heard me speak my language to my grandmother. There aren't that many native speakers of it here in the United States, less in Canada. It's a shame, but because of it, I made sure to learn and keep it fresh in my memory. Interacting more with English speakers makes that difficult. Except, of course, when talking with my grandmother."

Shiya flinched. "Your grandmother doesn't like me. I think I offended her when I didn't want the potion."

"Devil's club juice," he corrected. "Don't worry about it. She is set in her ways and is very traditional. Unlike me, she has no need to integrate with society and lives on the mountain. She comes down only to sell her wares."

Shiya thought she saw frustration in his expression. She patted his arm. "I know how that is. My mother had her ways too. It drove my dad nuts."

"Had?"

She kicked herself for mentioning her mother, not only because it hurt to remember and she still missed her after five years, but also because of the way her mother died. "She died when I was twenty-five."

"I won't push. I can tell it hurts." He tucked her into his embrace, and her eyes grew moist at the unexpected sensitivity. She let him hold her a heartbeat and then pulled away. Puffy red eyes weren't sexy.

"So what about your parents? Still alive? Do you have any siblings?" She started walking again, and he followed.

"Yes, my parents are alive. They, like my grandmother, don't come into the city or the borough often. I have many brothers and sisters."

"Many?"

"A few."

"What's a borough?"

He seemed to search his mind for the answer. "The county."

"Ah, okay."

He took her hand, and they continued down the trail. Someone had laid out planks to walk in the damper areas, and in a few flatter spots, patches of snow surprised her.

"So what about you?"

She looked up at him. "Me?"

"Yes, do you have family?"

"Oh, I keep forgetting Birk knows all this about me, but you and I are just getting to know each other. I have two sisters and a brother. My sisters are one year older and two. I guess you could say we're stepladder kids. My brother is five years older than Sakura."

His brows rose. "Sakura?"

"Yes." She rolled her eyes. "My mother was into the whole Japanese thing at the time Sakura was born. The word means 'cherry blossoms.' Do you know about sakura trees?"

"I can't say I do."

"They're beautiful, and so is my sister."

He tugged a lock of her hair, sending chills racing down her spine. "She's not the only one."

Shiya turned away. "You're flattering me."

He stopped her from walking and pulled her back to face him, trapping her hands between them. Kotori leaned toward her until their lips were less than an inch apart. "Is it flattery if it's true? Or are you questioning my motives?"

"I wouldn't presume, sir."

She stuck out her tongue, and he met it with his own. For a while, they danced that way, tongues swiping across each other, curling together without their lips touching. Kotori seemed to grow tired of that game, though, because he reached behind her head and drove her nearer. His mouth crushed hers in a desperate kiss, forcing her to tilt it back farther. When his hand came up her side and he pinched hard at her nipple, she cried out in ecstasy. His roughness turned her on like she never imagined such a thing would. He rolled the tiny bud between his fingers and tugged at it. A flood of cream wet her panties, and he growled low in his throat. Shiya was ready right there to take off her clothes and let him have it all, but Kotori pushed her away.

She stared at him, his big chest rising and falling with his harsh breathing. He ran a hand through the midnight curls, disordering them in the sexiest way she'd ever seen. She tucked her hands into her jacket pockets.

"We should keep moving, or you'll get cold," he said.

The words were almost angry, and she wondered what had gone wrong.

After some time, they fell into conversation again.

"What's your other sister's name? Is she also named after a tree?"

Shiya laughed. "No, but my mother kept the *S* theme. My middle sister's name is Shae."

"And your brother has an *S* name?"

"No, he was before the crazy naming scheme took hold." She laughed. "He's Kasen, and I can't imagine him soft enough to fall in line with matching names."

After she'd blurted out all their names, she wondered if it was wise. If Kotori had heard of the Keith hunters, he might put two and two together. Kasen was her father's name, and her brother a junior. Kasen Keith wasn't a common moniker by any means. While she worried over it, Kotori walked behind her in silence. She stumbled over a plank, and he caught her around the waist.

"I think we've gone far enough," he said. "The hike down the mountain is two hours. It might be better for you to take the tram back."

From the look of Kotori's powerful legs, she knew he would have no trouble, but as a city girl, hiking wasn't normally her thing, not in chilly weather anyway. She had enjoyed herself and told him so.

"You miss Birk?"

She smiled. "A little. Hey, can we visit his clinic and see him at work?"

Kotori hesitated, and she wondered if they had something to hide there. That might be good to look into. The correct procedure was to pass the info on to her brother or one of the other leaders if he wasn't available, but she hesitated. Things were going well between her and the guys, and that had nothing to do with her job. Maybe she needed to face the reality of the situation, but not yet.

"Okay, why not?" he agreed, and they started back.

When they were in the Bronco, Kotori called Birk, and left a message when he didn't answer. She noted the crease between his brows, but he didn't deny her. Tempted to tell him never mind since they didn't get the okay from Birk, she clamped her lips together. Her dad and Kasen would rake her over the coals if she let this opportunity pass her by. *Just think, what would Shae do?* Her confident and capable sister would reach over and put a hand on Kotori's thigh, giving him ideas of future pleasure, and the guy would let her lead him around by the nose, without her giving up the goodies. How the heck did one do that? Not that she wanted to hold the goodies back, of course.

The small building at the end of a side street seemed unassuming, yet cute, when they arrived. Where the slanted blue tiled roof met the eggshell wall, a sign read Rider Veterinary Hospital.

She turned to Kotori. "Wow, I thought it was a clinic, and he owns it?"

Kotori shrugged, and they walked inside. A receptionist greeted them with a smile, but when she saw Kotori, her face almost glowed. "Good morning, Kotori. Good to see you."

"Shannon," he murmured without enthusiasm. Shiya wondered if there was history there, but didn't say anything.

"We're here to see Dr. Rider. Is he in?"

Shannon's inquisitive gaze turned to her, but it swung back to Kotori as if she looked for an explanation from him. Before Kotori could say anything further, a door beside the desk opened, and a beautiful blonde stepped through. Behind her Birk appeared. The woman laid a hand on Birk's arm, talking to him in a low tone. From her flustered and eager bearing, she wanted Birk, and nothing in his reaction told Shiya the feeling wasn't mutual.

Shiya was too pissed off. She forgot to look around to see if she could pick up clues. She forced her gaze off Birk and scanned the room. Several people waited with pets in the reception area—dogs, cats, even birds, but no unusual animals. Maybe there was another location for the more exotic creatures native to Alaska.

Birk ended his conversation with the woman when a technician walked up with a caged cat. Birk escorted the woman closer to where they stood. "Let's try to avoid any more fights with porcupines, okay?"

Shiya winced. Poor kitty.

"Thanks, Dr. Rider." The woman pushed a card into his hand. "Give me a call anytime."

No the bitch didn't.

Shiya realized she must have stepped forward, when Kotori's hand flattened on her belly. His lips touched her ear. "Easy, little tigress. You can punish him later."

She smacked his hand away, but his words calmed her and had her trying to suppress a smile. Oh yeah, she would. Then she considered the ridiculousness of the situation. Birk would freely share her with Kotori, but she got an attitude when he considered another woman. Still, *he* agreed to share. She didn't, and they hadn't even slept together yet.

"Shiya," Birk said when he walked over to her, and she saw genuine pleasure in his gaze. He kissed her cheek and invited them to the back.

Shiya peered into every room as they headed to Birk's office. The small hospital included two examination rooms, a lab area, a pharmacy, a treatment area, and a surgical suite with several cages for the animals after an operation. They passed equipment in a small closet-sized room that looked like an X-ray machine, and Birk confirmed her thoughts.

In his office with the door shut, Birk perched on the side of his desk and held out his arms. Shiya hesitated.

"She's angry with you about the woman," Kotori supplied.

Shiya whirled on him. "Who asked you?"

Birk leaned forward, captured Shiya's hand, and dragged her into his embrace. She had to admit she loved the feel of his bunched muscles beneath her hands, but she wouldn't make it easy for him. She and Birk knew each other a little better than she knew Kotori, and she expected—well, she didn't know what she expected. Maybe she had no right to assume anything.

Then she considered if the woman was like them. Wouldn't they prefer a nonhuman lover to share? Had they ever had sex with a human? This whole affair had her head spinning, and figuring out the right path seemed impossible. Fight her head, fight her body, and . . . no, her heart had nothing to do with it.

"Hey." Birk touched a finger to her lips, and she turned her head. He turned it back toward him. "Look at me."

"Birk, I'm not here for games. I—"

"What are you here for?" He pinched open the buttons on her jacket. She wiggled in his hold, but he gripped her tighter. "Tell me, Shiya, why are you here?"

She had a moment of panic thinking he knew the real reason, but if he did, would he be opening her jacket the way he was? Would he push her blouse up to show her bra, and would he brush fingers along the valley between her breasts? She moaned when he did that, and he tugged at her bra as if he would raise it or drag it down. He did neither, but hooking his finger in the middle set her on fire. She didn't look up at him.

"I have to work a little while longer." He pushed a knee between her legs and drew her up along his hard thigh. She resisted humping it like the horny heifer she was. Birk raised her chin and kissed her lips. "However, tonight I want to be in your bed."

Why did it sound more like a command, or his informing her of where he would be tonight, like it or not? She licked her lips and nodded. "Fine, but I'm not sharing."

The card the woman had given him stuck out of his shirt pocket. She swiped it and crumpled it in her palm. Rather than display anger, Birk grinned, and his eyes flashed excitement.

"Whatever you want." He smacked her ass and released her. Shiya stepped over to Kotori and slipped her hand in his. He drew her to his side and wrapped an arm around her waist.

"What time, bro?"

Birk checked his watch. "Five? I need to see a few more patients. You two having fun without me?"

Shiya thought she saw a significant look pass between them, and Kotori raised his brows. "Don't worry. I won't eat her before you join us. After that, you're on your own if you're too busy."

"Hold on. You two are pretty confident," Shiya complained. Both men laughed, and Kotori ushered her out the door.

They spent the rest of the day wandering the city, with Shiya checking out every shop until Kotori dug in his boots and refused to visit another. They ate lunch together, and then he dropped her off at her room until it was time for them to meet later. She intended to get plenty of rest, because it was for sure Birk and Kotori would work her over that night, and she could not wait.

Chapter Four

At four, Shiya rose and showered. She wrapped a towel around herself and knotted it at the side of her breast. Then she checked her messages. Seeing a tick beside the voice mail emblem, she clicked that button and found she had three. Bypassing the ones from her dad and Joe, she chose Shae's.

"Hey, girl, call me. I want to know how the seduction is going. I also heard Joe's up there, and want to know if you're dealing or do I need to come bust his balls. He wants you back, you know. Call me!"

Shiya groaned. She didn't want to remember Joe was in town. She'd almost wiped the memory of him visiting her room out of her head. She couldn't blame Shae, though. Her sister cared about her emotional well-being.

She checked the time and figured she could afford to spend a few minutes on the phone. Just before she dozed off earlier, she'd texted both Kotori and Birk that they would have dinner in her suite tonight. She knew they would drew conclusions from that and look forward to it. Even as she thought of them, the unsettled feelings for Joe made her wonder if she should cancel.

She dialed Shae and waited for the call to go through. When Shae picked up, hearing her soft, yet confident voice soothed her somewhat.

"Hey, girl, what's up? How are things in chilly Juneau?"

"Chilly," Shiya responded.

"Wait, don't tell me your targets are playing hard to get. Wear something sexy with your legs or boobs hanging out. That will reel them in."

Why did their whole job sound so sexist all of a sudden? She didn't think the male hunters had to put it on display so obviously. Then again, most of them were sexy, so looking hot could be part of the job. No one ever said so outright. Her involvement in the fieldwork had been limited by her own decision.

"No, it's not like that, and I would freeze my butt off if I did that. The season is changing, and it's freaking cold. Why didn't I do this in summer?"

"You didn't have all your information together, and the witness took his time naming names."

Shiya sighed. All Shae said was true. "Anyway, they're into me."

"Of course!" Her sister whooped and then calmed down. "What's that I hear in your voice? Shiya Yvonne Keith, you better come out with it. Don't make me get on a plane and come down there—I mean up." She chuckled.

"You can't laugh when you're threatening someone." She considered whether she wanted to tell Shae about sleeping with Birk and Kotori, but thought better of it. Her sister might be sweet in most ways, but she hated shifters just like the rest of her family. Shae might kiss them—because something in the DNA made them all hot as hell—but she wouldn't spread her legs for any of them. "Joe came to see me."

"Old Joe." Shae sighed. "He doesn't know how to back off and let things be, and Dad's worse because he encourages him. I think he had visions of you two marrying and working together in the family business."

"Seriously?" Shiya grumbled. "I can choose my own husband. In fact, I'm not sure I want to get married—*ever*."

Shae's voice dropped low. "I know he hurt you, sweetie."

Shiya clenched her hands into fists. She shut her eyes. Okay, she was so screwed up.

"I-It was both of us, not just him. We didn't work out."

"Shiya, he used you to get next to Dad. I call that a scumbag wanting me to kick his balls into his throat."

"Now you sound like Sakura."

Shae made a noise of annoyance. "I can't touch that girl. She's evil."

Shiya laughed.

"What? She'll never get a man, hateful as she is."

"You know you wrong, right?" She couldn't help bursting out laughing because she felt the same about their older sister. "Sakura will find the one. I don't know about me, but then I'm not trying."

"Girl, you've had one guy—Joe—and he wasn't worth it. Sure he hung on for a while, still seeing you after Dad put him into leadership, but that was so he wouldn't get booted out of his cushy new position."

"Damn, you make it sound like no man would want me unless he has ulterior motives," Shiya snapped. "I happen to think Joe loves me."

Shae was silent, and Shiya wondered if she'd hung up. "Then why did you break up with him, honey? I'm sorry. I didn't mean to imply no one wants you. That's baloney because you're beautiful. I bet you have those animals eating out of the palm of your hand. Just be careful, Shiya, is all I'm saying. Joe was your first, so you don't have a lot of experience with guys. Shifters especially have sex drives out of this world. It's all I can do to make them keep it in their pants." Shiya heard the anger and annoyance in her sister's tone. "I handle them because I'm trained to, and I've been doing it for years. You be careful! Check in when you're supposed to, and above all else, do not go anywhere alone with them, not in your room and not to their house. Okay?"

Funny her sister should say those words as soon as a knock sounded at her door. Shiya hadn't ordered dinner nor put on any clothes. She sat on the side of her bed still in a towel. "Okay," she managed to tell her.

After a few more comments, Shae hung up, and Shiya dropped the phone on her bed. The knock came again. Would she go through with it and live a fantasy most women dreamed of, or would she call it off and tell her dad she needed to stay behind the computer screen because she couldn't keep her hands or her body to herself? *Yeah, not telling him that last part.*

She stood, checked that her towel remained secure, and strode into the living room, to the door. When she swung it open to reveal Birk and Kotori, she knew she would not back down from her decision. Not this century. "Hello, gentlemen. Care to come in?"

The two of them stepped through the doorway, and Birk handed her a bottle of wine. Shiya calmly thanked him and went to the kitchen area for glasses. She poured each a glass and one for herself.

Birk took a sip of the wine, his gaze sweeping her from head to foot. "I like the way you get down to business when you've made up your mind."

She put a hand on her hip. "I intended to be dressed and ready, but time got away from me. I never ordered food either."

"Who needs food when there's you to eat?" Kotori threw in, stalking closer.

She took a step back, searching her mental database. No shifters were known to eat humans, were they? The lust in both men's eyes told her she was on the menu, but not that kind of eating. A gush of desire led her to squeeze her legs together. Both of them lowered their attention to the hem of her towel as if on cue. Oh yeah, she'd made no mistake in her assessments.

She spun on her heel. "I'll be right back."

She zipped to her room and lotioned her body, then threw the towel aside to grab the dress she'd intended to wear. Yanking on a thong with one hand, she struggled to get her hair into some semblance of order with the other. In the end, she opted to pin it at the back of her head, stick a barrette in it, and call it a day.

When she returned to the living room, she went barefoot. No sense putting on shoes when they weren't going out, and she had nothing but the stylish heels the guys seemed to think were impractical. Two sets of eyes watched her as if she were prey crossing the living room to the table.

"Here's a listing of restaurants that deliver," she announced, "or did you have a specific place for us to order from?"

Birk strode over to her and took the listing from her hand. He laid it on the table and ran his fingers along her hip. "I preferred the towel—easier to remove—but the dress molds to your curves just right. *This*, however, won't do."

She stood there stunned when he reached up to her hair and took out the barrette and pins she had painstakingly put in.

"I like your hair down. You'll wear it that way for me?" He angled his mouth above hers, tempting her beyond reason. What the heck else was she going to say?

"Of course," she said in a breathy whisper.

"Good girl." Birk led her to the couch, where Kotori had taken a seat. He guided her to sit beside his friend, and then he took the spot on her other side. "Let's discuss things."

She raised her brows, peering from one to the other. "Things?"

Kotori nodded. "We need to know what you like, what you don't. Is there anything off-limits?"

Birk cut in with a hand on her inner thigh. He slid it higher until goose bumps rose on the sensitive skin, and she squirmed beneath his touch. "Are you a virgin or experienced?"

That question took her by surprise, not because she didn't think it should matter, but because Birk seemed excited with the prospect of her answer. She couldn't tell if he hoped she'd done it, or if he preferred her as a virgin so he could teach her.

She tried looking as self-assured as possible, crossing one leg over the other and taking up her wineglass for a sip. She leaned back, swirling the contents, and kept her attention on the burgundy liquid. "I'm not a virgin, but I've only been with one man."

Kotori closed the space between them until his massive thigh touched hers. Shiya's breath hitched, and her heart tried jumping from her chest. So much for appearing calm.

Her dark soon-to-be lover took the glass from her trembling fingers and raised her hand to nip her inner wrist. "Do you like to be spanked?"

She shivered. "I think I might like it. I haven't officially had it done."

"And what about anal?" Birk suggested. "Do you like it?"

"I've never tried it."

Birk undid the buttons on her dress and let it gap open a bit, revealing that she had elected not to wear a bra. He skimmed his hand over her nipple, pebbling the little bud. "And?" he demanded.

"I think I might try. I-I admit I'm nervous."

"We will teach you," Kotori assured her. "Oral?"

"Oh yes, giving and receiving."

"Mm, Shiya, you are a perfect little human, aren't you?" The deep rumble in Birk's voice washed over her. She leaned back against him, while Kotori pushed her dress up her thighs. Her pussy clenched knowing soon he would not only see it but touch her in the most intimate of ways.

Wait, did he call me a perfect little human?

Kotori's finger flicked her clit, swollen behind the material of her thong. She moaned.

"Easy, my friend," Birk told Kotori. "Shiya is different. We have to be sure about her."

She raised her chin to meet Birk's gaze. "I'm sure."

He kissed her, threading his tongue into her mouth. She parted her lips wider and tasted him with greedy hunger. Birk pulled her hand up to push into his hair. The murmur of sound he made with his throat didn't seem humanly possible. He liked her stroking her fingers through his locks.

Kotori tucked his hands under her knees and jerked her forward a little. The movement broke her and Birk's kiss, and she looked over at him. Kotori's unhappiness was clear at being told to wait while Birk went ahead and kissed her. She leaned up on her knees and gave him the same treatment. Their tongues met and curled together. Kotori's was so big it filled her mouth and sent tingles of pleasure to her core.

Unlike Kotori, Birk waited until they were done before he continued. The tent in his pants only belied his patient attitude. He drew her away from Kotori to sit down.

"Baby, my friend likes it rough. To please you, he can tone it way down."

Birk eyed Kotori. "But on the way over here, he also told me of your reaction when he pinched your nipple on the trail."

"Damn, do y'all tell each other everything?"

Birk whipped her onto his lap and raised her dress up to her waist. "Isn't it important for us to know if you like a little pain?"

That made her nervous, and a bit intrigued. She scooted off Birk's lap and stood up. Both men followed her movements as she raised the dress over her head and tossed it aside. She liked her figure okay because she worked to keep it, and her breasts were on the upper side of a C cup.

Both Birk and Kotori stared at her breasts, and then Kotori swore. She glanced at him and smiled. He'd noticed her thong panties. She turned to the side and let him look.

"All the way," Birk commanded.

Okay, Kotori might like it rough, but Birk enjoyed giving orders. She spun for him and waited for his approval.

"Take them off."

She put her hands to the band.

"No, wait."

She peered over her shoulder at him. Birk stood and loosened his belt. Her gaze flew to his face.

"Do you or don't you like it rough, Shiya? We need to know now before we start. We will always take our cues from you, and if you tell us to stop, we will, but if you say you're open to anything, we will do anything and everything in our enjoyment of that lovely body. Do you understand?"

She licked her lips. "I understand. I want all you have to offer me. If I don't like it, you'll know. But . . ." She hesitated.

Birk waited for her to speak again.

"I don't know you that well. I want to, but can we take it a little slower tonight?" She thought they would balk, but Birk held his hands out. She turned and took a few tentative steps toward him. He kissed her shoulder and her neck. His fingers skimmed over her hips, and he drew her closer until their bodies just touched. Kotori stood up and walked around behind her. When he dropped to his knees and pulled her thong down over her legs, her anticipation grew, but when he parted her cheeks and gave her a kiss back there, she went up to her toes and gasped.

"Mm, you like that," Birk whispered in her ear as if he knew what Kotori did. He nibbled her earlobe and sucked the skin at her neck between his lips. At the same time, he cupped her breasts and weighted them in his hands.

Behind her, Kotori rimmed her anus with a wet thumb and pushed against the barrier. She moaned, closing her eyes and clutching at Birk's shoulders. Weren't they going to take this slow?

In unison, both men stood back and removed the rest of their clothing. Shiya took her turn gawking at their incredible bodies. Skin drawn taut over sculpted muscle extended into the valleys and plains that made these men. Not an ounce of fat or imperfection met her hungry gaze. She took her time taking in Birk's chest down to his abs, all carved muscle. She continued down, and her mouth watered. His cock jutted from his body, reaching out toward her. The rigid shaft had to be a good eight inches with solid thickness. Her hands itched to hold him and play to her heart's content, but she spun to check out Kotori.

Like Birk, Kotori was built. The man towered above her, all chiseled steel. His wide chest tapered to narrow hips, and his abs couldn't get any more developed, with an eight-pack. When her gaze reached his cock, though, she shoved a fist into her mouth and just stared. Kotori's sheer girth would mean pain when he first entered her, and that was for sure. She swallowed. What caused her to sigh, somewhat in relief, was his length, not quite all that Birk sported. *Oh, but with how fat it is, he'll kill me.*

"Don't be afraid, Shiya," Birk said, pulling her to face him. "Kotori knows how to use it. He grabbed his own cock and stroked. "And so do I." He caressed her cheek with one finger and ran it over her mouth. He pushed the digit between her lips, and she knew what would come next. "Now, get on your knees and please your lovers."

When she didn't move right away, Kotori gave her ass a swat. She jumped from the sting, more shocking than it had been when Birk spanked her.

"Now," Birk ordered.

Kotori dropped a pillow from the couch on the floor for her to kneel on, and she sank to her knees. Birk spread his legs, still holding his cock in his hand. He grasped her chin, raised it, and tapped her lips with the tip. "Open."

She did as he wanted, and right away, the salty tang of precome coated her tongue. She licked more beading at the head, and Birk moaned. When she took him into her mouth, he knotted his fingers into her hair and slowly drove himself deeper, and then pulled back. He pushed in once more and then withdrew. Shiya took as much as she could, but Birk was too long to take all of him, and she knew nothing of deep throating a man.

After she'd been sucking Birk for a while, Kotori stood beside his friend. Birk slipped free of her mouth, and she looked up at her other lover. There was no way she could get him into her mouth.

"Suck it, Shiya," Birk commanded.

She leaned in and licked the tip. A hiss escaped between Kotori's teeth. She opened as wide as she could, but only the thick head slid past her lips. She gave him a hard suck, and a grunt tore from Kotori.

"Mm, yes, like that. Don't stop."

She took him into her hands and wrapped her fingers around his girth. Licking along the sides pleased him, so she explored lower. Remembering how he liked it rough, she tried giving his thin skin a tiny nibble, just enough to sting but not hurt. Kotori almost roared his pleasure.

Not to leave her first lover in the cold, she began stroking his cock while still licking and sucking Kotori. She massaged Birk's balls and then switched from one man to the other, back and forth. With the two men standing on each side of her, she brought their cocks close, but not touching, and licked both at the same time. She sucked on one head and then the other. Then she took a little of each on the sides of her mouth, placing pressure on their staffs with her lips. Birk and Kotori moaned her name and tilted their heads back.

Shiya raised Birk's cock and licked her way down from the tip to the base, following the bulging vein running its length. She switched to Kotori and turned her head sideways to give an open-mouth kiss that slid from the top all the way down his massive shaft. She gave him a small nip and then brought both shaft heads to her mouth to suck again.

Kotori twitched. He grabbed the back of her head and held it, so she knew he didn't want her to take him out of her mouth again. Building a steady rhythm, she pushed her tongue against the bottom side of their cocks and brought her lips down on top. Kotori twitched a second time, and she had seconds to realize what it meant before her mouth flooded with his come.

The thick liquid pooled on her tongue, and she swallowed it as more squirted on her cheek. Kotori had scarcely finished coming when Birk joined him.

Shiya didn't get to drink his because Birk pushed her back and took his cock from her mouth. He lowered it and let the cream shoot out onto her breasts while he watched. When he was done, he disappeared into the bathroom and came back with a towel to clean her off.

"Now, on the couch," he instructed.

She climbed up and lay on her back. Kotori stood beside her and placed a hand on her knee to pull her legs apart. She took in his beautiful body and marveled at how he'd already begun to grow hard again. Birk positioned himself at the end of the chair, facing her. He hoisted her hips and propped her ass on a pillow. Shiya bit her lip. Her pussy clenched in anticipation. She already knew she was drenched down there, and they were about to help it along.

Chapter Five

Birk was the first to dip his head between her legs. She moaned when his tongue teased her clit. He flicked it and circled the small bud, then sucked it into his mouth. Shiya shoved a fist between her lips and thrashed at the sensations. Kotori laid a heavy hand on her belly to hold her down.

"I think she likes it," he commented. His voice, deep and scratchy as if he weren't used to using it, made her look at him, but Kotori had already dropped to his knees and lowered his head as well. He thrust Birk back, and she thought they might get into a scuffle, but Birk gave his friend space.

Kotori used his wide tongue to swipe her pussy from the base to the top. He didn't linger at her clit, but went down a second time to delve between her folds. She screamed in pleasure and tried to raise her pussy toward him. The hand he used to keep her immobile checked all movements.

"Kotori," she moaned.

Her lover gazed up at her, his eyes narrowed, and she saw the danger in the depths, just as she'd seen when she first met him. His hunger seemed to stretch out to engulf her. Leaning over her side, he grasped both her legs and thrust them higher. The shift caused her folds to separate, and he grunted at the sight. He licked her again, making sounds with his mouth that made her dizzy.

"Switch places with me," Birk asked Kotori, and they swapped, with Kotori down below and Birk at her side. As soon as he was in position, Birk placed a thumb at the top of her pussy, just above the hood covering her clit, and he massaged the area in a circle. Shiya squirmed.

"W-What are you doing?" she whimpered.

Birk didn't pause in his ministrations. He kept his thumb moving and bent to begin sucking her clit again. Kotori joined him with sticking his tongue up her channel. The two areas pleasured at the same time had Shiya crying out their names, and when her first orgasm came, it exploded with such power, vibrations pulsed through her entire being.

When she calmed, Birk and Kotori sat up. Birk rubbed her belly. "Good?"

"Yes," she murmured because she had no strength to speak louder.

Birk stood. "I think I'd like to continue this in that Jacuzzi you have in there." He raised his brow. "Are you game?"

Was he kidding? "Yes."

Birk instructed her to get it ready, and she left the room to do his bidding. Behind her, she heard them whispering and wondered what they were talking about, but it didn't matter. So far, sharing two men was incredible, and she wanted everything else it came along with.

She ran the water in the large round tub and added a generous amount of bubble bath. When the men came in, Birk laid something on the sink, and then the two of them offered her a hand to help her up the step and into the tub. She settled in the warm depths and watched with interest as each man came in after her.

Birk moved to one side of the tub, while Kotori occupied the side opposite. Shiya took up space between the two of them. Her foot brushed a hard leg, and she used it to run up and down the length, watching for whichever man it was. Kotori's hands snaked out, and he drew her to him. His lips claimed her mouth in a rough kiss. When he let her up for a breath of air, he moved his hands from her waist to her nipples and pinched. She moaned at the sweet agony and arched into his touch.

"Come here, Shiya," Birk said. Kotori released her, and she answered Birk's call, waiting in front of him. He took the sponge on the side of the tub, along with shower gel and squeezed some out. Once the sponge softened with suds, he handed it to her. "Wash me."

Shiya didn't hesitate. Running the sponge over his skin turned her on, especially when she got to clean his chest, trace the shape of his big shoulders and muscular arms. She dipped beneath the water's surface, and Birk snagged her wrist to make her wash his cock. A ping of desire stirred between her legs each time he guided her hand up and down the length of his shaft. When she thought it couldn't possibly need any more, Birk took the sponge from her hand and wrapped her fingers around his cock. The throbbing hardness attested to him being ready to take her, and she wished he would do it now.

"Wash Kotori," he ordered.

In part, the command disappointed her. She wanted to be taken, and from the light in Birk's eyes, he knew it as well. He held back, and she knew he did it on purpose. She considered two playing that game, but obeyed him instead. She liked how things were going so far. Challenging her lovers with her strong will could come another night.

Kotori's body excited her the same as Birk's did. Just like his friend, he guided her in washing his cock, but he took the sponge from her fingers right away. She had to clean his taut bronzed skin with her hands from the start. When she finished with his cock, Kotori placed her hand on his balls and covered it with his own. He made her squeeze, and he covered her mouth, growling between kisses.

"Why do I have the feeling you can never get enough?" she asked him.

He raised her at the hips out of the water, and goose bumps formed on her skin from the chill air. With amazing strength, Kotori held her in front of him and sucked her clit. She braced herself on his shoulders, crying out. He stuck his tongue up her channel and wiggled it around. Trembling in her limbs left her weak. She held on, at his mercy until he had his fill.

Just before Shiya reached a second orgasm, Kotori leaned back. She could have wept. He let her down slowly, and behind her Birk stood. He reached for a condom packet, which was the thing he'd placed on the sink. After ripping the plastic open, he rolled the covering onto his cock. He crooked a finger in her direction. "Come here."

When she reached him, he lifted her up to the edge of the tub and parted her thighs.

Shiya panted and braced herself, hands at her sides.

"Are you ready?"

She raised her chin. "Oh yes, baby, give it to me."

Birk grinned. He captured her heels, lifted them, and thrust forward. She gasped and closed her eyes as her pussy walls expanded around him. "Not a virgin" meant nothing when it came to Birk's size, and the feeling sent her over the top. He jerked her legs higher to rest her heels on his shoulders and thrust deeper. She cried out his name. When her muscles relaxed enough, he began an easy pump in and out of her pussy.

Kotori wandered over and bent to kiss her. She curled her tongue with his, and he moved around behind her so he could take her weight. When she rested on his chest, he took her hand to place on his cock. Behind her back, Shiya stroked him. She rubbed a thumb over the rounded head and slid lower to play with his balls. All the while, Kotori nibbled on her neck and pinched her nipples. She'd never had so much attention before, and feeling Birk slide his amazing shaft inside of her as Kotori kissed her and teased her nipples took away all rational thought. She never wanted it to end.

Birk stopped moving. He pushed in to the hilt and waited. "Hold on to me, baby."

She lowered her legs, but he didn't pull out. Then she leaned forward and put her hands on his arms. Kotori stood to put a condom on. Shiya clenched her teeth together.

"Shh, it's going to be fine," Birk told her.

His change from cold commands to gentle comfort pleased her. Both attitudes appealed, in that he knew when to use which persona. She tucked her head low and nuzzled into the base of his neck.

When Kotori was ready, they switched places, but Birk hesitated. "Wait, I want her relaxed more to take you."

Birk took off his condom and disposed of it. He stood her in the center of the bath and began washing her from head to toe. When he was done, Kotori waited with a towel, and she stepped into his arms. He carried her to the bedroom and laid her on the bed. Birk followed and took the position at her side.

Kotori climbed onto the bed and kneeled below her. He grabbed her legs and dragged her toward him. Shiya's breath came in short bursts at the sight of his cock. He pushed it to her hole and pressed forward, and she clenched the sheets under her fingers.

"No, Shiya, relax," Birk told her. "He's not going to be rough this time around." Birk cast his friend a stern look.

"Do it," she begged, wanting to feel him. She wanted the ache. When Kotori still hesitated, she put a heel on his shoulder and reached for his cock. The head threaded in, so tight it seemed like it would never fit. Kotori thrust forward. She caught her breath, and then his dick sank in inch after slow inch. If she said it didn't hurt, she would be lying, but the sensation mingled with the feeling of overfullness and bliss.

Shiya coaxed Kotori's shaft to go deeper inside of her. She raised her hips to take him and lowered them when he'd gone as far as he could. Her pussy contracted around him, drawing on his shaft, and felt so amazing she pleaded with him not to stop. Kotori dropped over her, his arms locked at her sides with her legs over them, and he picked up the pace. He pounded his thick cock home, and each time, a growl erupted from his throat.

She pulled her knees higher, loving the invasion. "Mm, it's too much, but I don't want it to stop."

"You're so damn tight."

"I'm sorry," she moaned.

"Don't be."

He pounded into her over and over. Shiya grew light-headed. The pleasure was too much, and she pushed at his chest. Kotori pulled out, and Birk, wearing another condom, slipped into her. Tag-teaming, they wore her little pussy out. When it was Kotori's turn again, he sat back and raised her up to sit on his lap. She encircled his neck with her arms, and he held her ass in a viselike grip so she didn't come down too fast. He raised her up and lowered her at lightning speed. Her breasts bounced over his chest, scraping her nipples. She screamed in excitement. Birk slid up behind her and reached between them to pinch her clit. The friction of Kotori's cock inside her and Birk pinching her bud brought her to another orgasm. She collapsed on Birk's chest when it ended.

Kotori tugged her away from his friend, not allowing her to rest. He never lost their connection as he drove his cock deep inside of her. Each thrust accompanied him squeezing her ass and fingering her rear entrance. When Kotori jerked, she knew he was ready. Seconds later, he let go of a long, satisfied moan. Birk pulled her free of his arms and laid Shiya on the bed while Kotori rose from it. Birk stretched the length of his body over hers and ran a hand along her outer thigh. They stared into each other's eyes, and Shiya felt herself becoming lost.

"Are you too sore for a little more?" he asked.

She almost fainted from the question, but she shook her head. "No."

He eased his cock inside of her and took his time, gliding in and out. Slow and easy, their bodies came together and drifted apart. A tormenting pleasure began in Shiya's core and steadily grew. She buried her face in Birk's neck. He held her tighter to him, and just when she came, he matched it, a tremor vibrating his limbs that touched hers. They both sighed when it ended, and Shiya found she couldn't keep her eyes open as she drifted off to sleep.

Shiya opened her eyes to a dark room. Birk and Kotori lay on either side of her, and she remembered how, while she slept, one or the other laid a heavy arm over her waist or slung a leg across hers. She'd had to thrust them away because she felt like they crushed her. At first she thought the two men slept like the dead in how still they were, but as soon as she put a hand up to rub her eyes, Kotori rolled over toward her, and Birk spoke.

"Okay?" he asked. "Not too sore?"

"I'm fine." She sat up, but Birk rested a hand on her arm.

"I want—*we* want—to say something to you."

Birk swung his feet over the side of the bed and clicked the lamp on. He seemed to have no compunction about being naked, but she pulled a sheet up over her. "Go ahead."

"I'll take a shower and dress first." He stood and disappeared into the bathroom.

Nervousness stirred in her stomach. What could they have to say? Did they not enjoy themselves last night? No, that couldn't be it. The men had let her sleep a short while and then woke her to go at it again. Their appetites were unbelievable, and she'd found it hard to keep up. Yet, every touch sent her into the stratosphere, so she didn't mind.

When Birk vacated the bathroom, Kotori took his turn. Birk walked to the living room to retrieve his and Kotori's clothes and returned to dress where she lay. Once again, she admired his body, taking in the valleys and plains, the corded muscle and sinew. When he yanked his boots on, his arm muscles bulged, and she sighed, remembering how they felt wrapped around her.

At last, they were both dressed, and Shiya had made no attempt to rise from the bed. She scooted up near the top and clutched the sheet under her arms. When Kotori eyed the imprint of her nipples behind the thin material, she crossed her arms. The man was impossible.

"So what's this about?" she said, hoping it wasn't something bad.

Birk leaned against the wall, arms folded. He opened the blinds and peered out as if he had nothing better to do with his day other than to watch the water. Shiya swung her gaze from first one man to the other. Kotori appeared content to let Birk head the conversation.

She opened her mouth to prompt Birk, but when he spoke, she snapped her teeth together so hard it shot a clang of pain through her head.

"You know what we are, Shiya."

The bottom dropped out of her world. He couldn't mean what she thought. No, he meant . . . what? "What you are?"

Birk sneered. "Let's not play any more games. You know Kotori and I are shifters, and we know what you are."

Human? Not a Keith. She pushed her way to the edge of the bed and stood to wrap the sheet tighter around her figure. Shuffling through all of the training, all the information crammed into her head over the weeks before she came here, she searched for what occurred next in a situation like this. The answer should be right there, engraved on her memory the way her dad lectured, but fear had wiped the canvas clean. With a glance, she checked the nightstand for her cell phone, but too late remembered she'd left it in the other room. Stupid move. No, it had been stupid to sleep with them.

Play dumb. "Just what do you think you know about me, Birk?"

He crossed the room in two or three strides. She backed up and hit the nightstand, knocking the lamp over. Kotori stood by, out of nowhere, to catch it and set it upright. Birk frowned down at her. "I thought we agreed no more games. If you're afraid of us, why did you have sex with us?"

Shiya stood straighter, hands on her hips. "Why are you so damn angry all of a sudden? Oh, I get it, all the charm flew out the window after you got what you wanted last night!"

His nostrils flared, and his hot gaze raked her from head to foot. "I can have any woman I want. It doesn't have to be you."

The crack of her hand slapping his face punctuated the air. Birk didn't move. A muscle twitched in his jaw.

"Feel better?" he said in a low tone.

She scowled at him. "Okay, I know you're shape-shifters."

"And you're a Keith," Kotori added. "From a family of shifter hunters."

Oh hell, so they did know. From the looks of it, they'd known from the beginning. Her family had hatched a plan for her to seduce them, and at the same time, they'd intended to draw her in.

She rubbed moist palms down her legs. "So what does this mean? You're kidnapping me to draw my dad to Juneau?"

"Interesting," Kotori muttered. "If we didn't have a plan like that, you would have given us the idea."

Shiya swore. "What then?"

Birk stepped closer. The heat from his body permeated her sheet, and even while she feared him in this state, she remembered how tender he had become several times during their time together. She recalled his funny jokes while they spoke online, the ones he told well and the ones he screwed up. They'd laughed, but that could be the charmer in him, a natural ability they all had to capture their prey.

"All of us have heard of you," Birk told her.

She lit on the word. "All?"

"Shifters in the United States."

Her research showed there were whole families of shifters, and some who were rare, producing one or two every so often. The time span might be a generation, or it might be a century. She knew that there might be shifters to come who hadn't been born yet. Their fight spanned over generations of Keiths and would likely go on into the future.

Kotori's voice broke through her reverie. "I want to know why you slept with us. As you've no doubt checked into who we are, we've done the same with your family. Like shifters, you close ranks and squash information that might leak out about your methods."

Birk picked up the conversation. "You use beautiful women to lure the shifters into trusting you. I thought it wouldn't lead this far. After all, the most common knowledge about the Keiths is that they think all shifters are killers. Yet, your men send the women in to fuck them without qualms."

"You don't know what you're talking about!" He leaned over her, but at that point, she would not back down. He made it sound like she and her sisters were whores, and he knew what he could do with his superior attitude. "You think you're better than us? You and Kotori were right there with me in bed, and you knew who I was, just like you said. You can say what you want about me, but you're going to take back insinuating my sisters are whores. They do not sleep with the men."

"There again, Shiya, why did you sleep with us?"

She saw he didn't want to let it go, and Kotori, standing next to him, was in total agreement. What difference did her answer make since they'd already made their minds up about her character? If they knew all along, why did they sleep with her? The answer came to mind as soon as she formed the question. As shifters with a high sex drive, they didn't care who shared their bed. Any woman would do, and she'd seen evidence of that at Birk's office when he accepted that blonde's card. A pang of jealousy hit her, but she tamped it down.

"I want you both to leave. You're no longer welcome." She stepped around Birk and squeezed by Kotori to get to the door. In the front room, she held the door open, waiting for them.

Birk walked up and put his hand on the knob. "We're not done here. You do not get to dismiss me."

When he slammed the door, she stumbled away from him in alarm, but before she could speculate on whether they intended to kill her, the door burst open again. Birk moved seconds before it did and pulled Shiya out of the way. She cried out at the sudden sound and the fact that Joe stood in the entryway.

"Get your hands off of her, *now*," Joe barked.

"Joe, what are you doing here?" Shiya thought to defuse the situation, but she realized she helped nothing wedged against Birk's chest, his hands still around her waist, and her sheet slipping dangerously low over her breasts. She struggled to get out of Birk's hold, and he let her go after holding on for a while as if he sought to piss Joe off.

"Who are you?" Kotori demanded, and Shiya glanced at him. His eyes didn't look right, and she worried he was about to change.

"Look, everybody calm down." Her hands shook as she held them up, and both Birk and Joe seemed to notice.

"Shiya, go to the bedroom," Joe commanded. "I'll take care of this."

"You'll take care of what?" Birk demanded.

He stepped around Shiya to get to Joe, but Joe had been taught to strike hard and fast. Delays would get a person dead. He produced a weapon she knew well because she had bought it for him. The eight-inch steel blade was half serrated on the top and sharp enough to cut through wood—or bone. She'd had the handle customized with a bright red grip, Joe's favorite color, and his name carved at the end.

Shiya ran her hands through her untidy hair, only now realizing she looked a hot mess. "Joe, what are you doing? You know you don't handle this kind of thing here. It's too dangerous."

"You want me to wait until they drag you out in the forest to eat you, Shiya?"

"Joe."

He lunged at Birk, but Birk parried the attack with the flat of his hand, knocking Joe's hand away. Her ex winced in pain, but to his credit, he didn't drop the weapon. He came at Birk again, jabbing with his knife, but when Birk went to block, Joe dropped low and kicked out. His foot slammed into

Birk's legs, and her lover hit the floor. Joe sprung up from his crouch and swung his arm to drive the knife into Birk's chest, and Shiya screamed. She ran forward to somehow stop Joe from killing Birk, but in the next instant, Kotori plowed into Joe, sending him and his knife flying. Kotori's growl didn't sound human as he stalked over to Joe. He jerked her ex up from the floor and dangled him from a powerful fist wrapped around his neck. Shiya saw the life leaving the man and knew if she didn't do something, he would die. Birk, picking himself up from the floor in obvious disgust that he'd let a human get the drop on him, made no move to stop it.

She ran over and grabbed Kotori's arm. "Stop, Kotori, please. Don't kill him."

Kotori snarled down at her, his eyes jet-black with little white showing. Fear stirred in her belly, but she refused to back away. Somehow she didn't think he would hurt her, or he already would have.

"Don't do this." She stood on tiptoe to reach up to his hand holding Joe in its iron grip. No amount of prodding could open his fingers. "Birk, make him stop! He's killing him."

"What do I care if another human dies, Shiya? He's one of you, isn't he? A Keith?"

"No, he's not. He works for my dad, but he's not related."

Shiya didn't know where Joe got the second weapon. The smaller knife, no longer than the palm of a woman's hand, swiped over Kotori's arm, cutting deep. Kotori drew back as blood gushed from the wound. He dropped Joe on the floor, who gasped and choked trying to drag in air to fill his lungs.

"Seems this man wants to die," Kotori spat and started toward Joe. Shiya darted into his path and held out her arms.

"He's my protector. It's his job to look out for me. Just, please, get your arm taken care of. If you two go like I asked you to, no one else has to get hurt."

"I'm her fiancé," Joe said in a raspy tone.

Both shifters froze. Shiya rolled her eyes. *Seriously, Joe? Jealousy now, when Kotori almost snapped your neck?*

"Be quiet," she demanded. "If you hadn't jumped the gun in the first place, none of this would have happened."

She expected Birk to accuse her of not only sleeping with the enemy like a two-bit whore, but also not respecting the commitment he thought she had to Joe. He said nothing. Rather, he strolled to the door, still standing open, and left. Kotori grabbed a towel for his arm and followed his friend, shutting the door behind him. Shiya took in the destroyed state of the lock and recalled the way the door wobbled now on its hinges. How the heck would she explain it to the manager? She closed her eyes and sank to the floor. A raging headache pulsed behind her eyes. The last twenty-four hours had gone from amazing to a nightmare, and it had all started to go wrong when she elected to veer off the path set before her.

"Shiya," Joe called out behind her.

She twisted around to look at him and took in the ugly purple bruises beginning to form on his neck. She wondered about Kotori's injury and hoped no major arteries had been cut. Would the hospital be able to help him? Or would Birk treat him in secret?

"Shiya!"

"What!"

"I will have to report this to Kasen and your dad."

She swore. Like she would ever marry this bastard in a million years. If he loved her, he would cover it all and say something went wrong, not that she screwed up. Well, she didn't need his help. She could explain it to her dad. Not about the sex, but about misjudging Birk and Kotori. That everyone would know she wasn't cut out for the field was fine. She never wanted to do it again, and her experience with Birk and Kotori could remain an insane memory—one that would fade over time into something unreal.

Chapter Six

Shiya stood over her baggage, staring as if it would pack itself. She had decided to leave, to go back to San Diego and tell her dad she'd washed out. He'd be disappointed, but the situation couldn't be helped. Her cell phone rang, and she picked it up to check the display. The muscles in her stomach tightened as she punched the connect button.

"Hey, Kasen."

"Do you know where Marine Way and Franklin is?"

She thought about it and remembered that was near the Red Dog Saloon, close to where the Juneau Public Library was located. She'd walked all along that area with Birk and Kotori. "Yes, I know."

"Be there in forty-five minutes." He hung up, and she frowned. Who the hell did he think he was? She didn't answer to Kasen. Well, not directly. Her dad had given her special permission to handle this job, and he did not say Kasen would be her leader.

Shiya examined her outfit, jeans and layered tops that she could remove if the weather turned a bit warmer. She decided she didn't need to change, and

Kasen didn't warrant a special outfit either way.

After checking the clock on the nightstand, she figured she had enough time to complete her packing. While she did so, she thought about why Kasen had come down from Anchorage. Joe must have followed through with his threat to report what happened with the guys. The question remained what Kasen felt about it. Would he let it go and agree with her going home?

She left the room, eyeing the handwork of the locksmith who had fixed her door. Not more than a couple hours passed before it was done, and the relief at not being tossed out on her ear had lifted a weight from her shoulders.

When she reached the street, Joe met her and walked along beside her. She frowned at him. "I guess I have you to thank for arranging to get the door fixed? You moved fast. What did you tell the inn manager to keep them from throwing me on the street?"

For a moment, Joe gave her a blank stare. He glanced over his shoulder toward the room, and then his face cleared. "Oh, uh, yeah, it was nothing. Don't worry about it."

"I do worry about it, because I don't want to owe you, Joe, and we still haven't talked about you claiming to be my fiancé. We're not involved, and we never will be again."

He slowed his gait, but she kept her speed. When he realized she wouldn't slow down, he jogged to walk beside her again. "Can you stop a minute, Shiya?"

"No, I'm meeting Kasen."

"Shiya." He grabbed her arm, but she shook him off and whirled on him. "What's your problem?"

"What's yours?" She glared at him, hands on her hips. "You expected me to thank you for telling Kasen what happened, that I failed? What, I was supposed to get back with you so you can tell my dad at least one plan went right—the one *you* orchestrated? I know, you thought you'd give this as evidence of why I should stay in the office and not do fieldwork, that you're a hero because you saved his daughter from the big bad bears!"

The incredulity in his expression served to piss her off even more because she knew he wasn't real. He reached out to touch her arm again, but she scowled so hard, he withdrew as if she'd tried to bite him.

"Shiya, I hate that you think of me that way. Wasn't I there for you?"

"Weren't you there for every dinner party my father threw?" she countered.

"Your dad invited me as your man, and as one of his leaders. Everyone else came, and you don't think they had ulterior motives. Why is it so hard for you to believe I love you?"

She shook her head sighing. "I believe you love me, Joe, I really do—in your own way. But you spent more time talking to me about what my dad said or did. You asked me more times than I can count what I thought he wanted. When I didn't know, you told me to ask him and let you know. But you want to know what the real kicker is?"

He compressed his lips, and red stained his handsome face. "I think you've said enough."

"No, not yet." She moved closer to him and raised her chin. "The real treat is that you always preferred Shae."

Joe's eyebrows disappeared into his hairline.

"Oh yeah, Kasen was kind enough to tell me *after* I let you into my bed. He said you were joking around with the guys, like y'all do, and you said the real beauty in the family is Shae because she's got a great combination between Shiya's sweetness and Sakura's ability to kick ass. She will make a man a great wife one day." To her disgust and anger, tears filled her eyes.

"Shiya, I—"

"What? You're going to say Kasen lied? Go ahead, tell me how he lied, Kasen, who doesn't give a crap who he hurts when he has something to say. You know what else?"

"Damn it, Shiya, that's enough!"

She went on like he hadn't spoken. "He said, 'But aside from that, he's a good man. Fights well and gets the job done. Wish he was black, but whatever, you should keep him.' As if my future husband should be a man who fights well and gets the job done, nothing else being important." She poked Joe in the chest and leaned in close to his face so he wouldn't miss her seriousness. "The next time you decide to claim a woman as your fiancée, choose someone else, because it damn sure won't be me. Oh, and Shae wouldn't touch you if you were the last man on earth."

Shiya swung on her booted heel and strode away. That conversation was the last she would have with Joe. For years, she'd been a fool, accepting his mess because he was her first and because she loved him, but she deserved better than he had to give. When he showed up in Juneau, she had a moment of weakness because of fear of something new and because of how she still felt about him. No more.

She checked the time. Joe had made her ten minutes late, and Kasen's mood would likely reflect it. She picked up the pace and soon came to the street where he said to meet him. Pedestrians strode all around Kasen, but her brother stood stock-still, legs apart, arms folded over a muscular chest, and head bowed. Intimidated glances were tossed his way because of the frown on his face, but he didn't appear to notice. Kasen was the second most single-minded man she knew, the first being her father. He had one goal in life, and that encompassed wiping out every shifter in existence.

She'd always been surprised that he had time to find a wife and have a son of his own. Before she left San Diego, there were rumors his wife was pregnant again, with the oldest aged two, but neither Kasen nor Sheila had confirmed yet.

"Hey, bro," she called when she drew close enough. "How's it going?"

He looked up and raised a single brow, something only Kasen could do. A scar lined the right side of his jaw where a tiger shifter once got the better of him. A matching set stretched across his chest. They had almost lost him, but the experience made Kasen harder—and meaner.

"Should you really be smiling at a time like this? Two confirmed—" He scanned the area around them. "Let's walk."

Shiya hurried to catch up with him as he started off. He didn't slow his gait at all to match hers. Maybe this was payback for her treatment of Joe earlier, or maybe rudeness ran in her family. They continued in silence for another few blocks, and then Kasen led her into a less populated area where they could speak more freely. He faced her, and she waited for his tirade. When he didn't speak for a while, she took the plunge.

"I'm sorry. I screwed up. I guess I'm not meant for fieldwork, or I need to shadow Shae or Sakura to get how it's done." She spread her hands to the side. "I don't think I have that natural thing, that seduction ability that they have."

"Are you serious?" he snapped.

"Thanks, but—"

"I think you forgot who you are, Shiya." While his words might hint at being a compliment, his tone of voice and the anger burning in his eyes told her she disgusted him. "You're a Keith, and it's time you start acting like one."

"Everbody's not like you, Kasen. Besides, I'm damn good at what I do, gathering research, talking to people—"

"On the phone," he interrupted. "On the computer." His nostrils flared. "You fucked up the relationship with Joe, and the first chance you get, you whore yourself out to a couple of animals that aren't even human."

She gasped. So Joe did tell him she slept with Birk and Kotori. Once again, she kicked herself for doing it at her place, and for that bastard Joe probably standing in the bushes watching her let them in. While she knew it was more than just her jumping into bed with Birk and Kotori, Joe's attitude and her brother's words had her feeling like what he accused her of, but she would not give him the satisfaction of knowing he made her feel that way.

"Don't get all holier than thou on me," she snapped. "Everybody knows how wild you were before you met and married Sheila."

"Human is the operative word here. *Human.* Like I said, you forgot where you came from. Shae and Sakura would never sleep with a shape-shifter. They'll be sickened to know you did."

Shiya crossed her arms over her chest and looked away from him. She refused to be goaded into begging him not to tell the others. He could do what the hell he wanted, and all of them could think what they wanted.

When she ignored him, Kasen seemed to calm down. He reached into his coat pocket and pulled something out she didn't see. He paced past her, but she stayed facing the way she was. The next thing she knew, pain erupted from several points on her head. Kasen had grabbed her hair, knotting his fingers in it, and gave it a sharp yank. She grasped his hands, crying out in pain. No matter how hard she tried to get free, he held on. The more she struggled, the more he pulled, until she stopped resisting.

"Let me go, Kasen. I don't want to fight you."

He laughed, a harsh sound that grated on her ears. "*You* fight *me*? That's funny." He held up his other hand, and she just caught the glimpse of a picture. He jerked her head around to see it clearly. "Look at it and remember who you are, bitch."

Shiya cried out again, and tears sprung to her eyes and spilled down her face. "Why do you have that?"

"To remind me," he snarled in her ear, "that the *things* we're dealing with aren't to be tolerated or made into friends. They aren't potential fuck buddies. They are the enemy."

Shiya lowered her gaze from the picture, but her brother gave her hair another yank.

"Look at it! See in detail what they did to our mother, how they ripped her body to shreds and left her for dead. Animal attack, the police said. Yeah, it was an animal attack, all right, a calculated murder. He hunted her for days, and when he caught up, he killed her. Not right away, though. No, he made her suffer for a while, bleeding to death."

"Stop." Her voice came out hoarse.

"Why? So you can keep the rosy picture you have in your head of those two polar bears? No, you're going to do what you came here to do, and me and my men are going to do what we do."

Shiya had had enough. She drove the side of her fist into her brother's testicles and stomped on his instep. His hold loosened, and she moved out of reach, both hands up to defend herself if need be.

"Damn it, Shiya," he roared, bent over and holding his junk.

She glared at him. "Oh, you can hurt me, but I can't hurt you?"

"You're going to pay for that."

"Why don't I ask Dad if it's okay for you to manhandle me, no matter what decisions I've made."

He paced back and forth a few steps, limping and muttering. When the pain seemed to have lessened, he straightened and then spotted the picture of their mother lying on the ground. Shiya averted her gaze from it without taking her eyes off Kasen, but he didn't attempt to approach her. She knew she didn't stand a chance against him in a normal fight. Hell, getting the drop on him when he least expected it had proved unsuccessful every other time, but she figured the subject itself—their mother's death—got to him as much as it did her, maybe more.

"It's over. Since Birk and Kotori know I'm a Keith, and they know we're hunters, I don't see any reason to continue this farce."

Her brother's nostrils flared. He tucked the picture into his coat. "*You* wouldn't. Nothing's over. You're going to continue as you were."

Shiya's eyes widened. She could not believe him. Did he care so little about her that he didn't mind Birk and Kotori killing her? He didn't get to burst in when they least expected it. So what? Kasen needed to get over himself.

"I guess you don't see how much they hate me? They'll kill me on sight."

"This is why men use you, Shiya."

She flipped him off, and he jerked her closer, his fingers biting into her arm.

"Kasen."

"You *will* respect me, Shiya."

She said nothing, and he shoved her away from him.

"If they wanted you dead, you already would be. Ever think of that?"

She blinked at him, and he swore, pinching the bridge of his nose.

"The one thing in common among all shifters, no matter their species, is what?"

"High sex drive?"

"That, and?" he demanded.

She searched her mind for information. Rubbing the spot where her brother had grabbed her, she ran through everything she knew, but none of it applied to her.

"Why don't you try spelling it out since I'm not getting it?"

"A mate."

She blinked again.

"Those two beasts have marked you as their mate. You obviously don't know it, and sometimes even the shifter doesn't recognize it. They knew who you were from the beginning. By their laws, they should have killed you. Even if you do nothing else, they will come to you—here or in San Diego. They will find you and make you theirs because, in their minds, you are their mate."

"That's BS," she snapped. "They hate me." Birk and Kotori had told her they'd shared women before. She had no reason to think she, above all others, was special, and Kasen and his notions could accept it.

"Who do you think fixed your door, Shiya?"

"How did you know about that?"

"*Who?*" he insisted.

"Joe? You?"

He said nothing.

When she delayed letting the manager of the inn know about the damage, she did so because she needed to make preparations if they pressed charges or if they just tossed her out. When the locksmith came and fixed everything, she thought they'd found out and just dealt with it. She had been ready to inform all her online buddies about the inn to choose when in Juneau. Then Joe claimed responsibility, and she let the matter drop. Now, Kasen was telling her Birk and Kotori made the arrangements.

"I don't understand why you're pushing this either way. Even Joe can attest that both Birk and Kotori are shifters. All you have to do is . . ." Pain tightened her chest, making it hard to breathe. She waved a hand like the rest didn't need to be said, but her brother cast her a knowing look that pissed her off. She turned away from him.

"I want them all."

She peered back at him. "What are you talking about?"

"Mother, father, sisters, brothers, aunts, uncles, and cousins. Every single person in their families."

Shiya's mouth went dry. "Y-You can't be serious, Kasen."

"Oh, I'm dead serious. They're not of the human race. That means killing them is no different than hunting wild game and putting one between its eyes."

His deep hatred was palpable, weighing her down until she panted. "You know some of them are not shifters. In fact, most aren't."

He nodded. The gleam in his eyes terrified her more than any physical assault he had done so far. "We've been going at this all wrong. We know that a few generations in the future, any shifter's family can, and does, produce new shifters. So we end up having to go back over the same territory. If we kill every one of them, we destroy the gene."

Horror clogged Shiya's throat, making it difficult to speak. "But they're innocent."

"No carrier of the shifter gene is innocent!"

"Dad can't agree—"

"Oh, he agrees. In fact, he commended me, said he doesn't know why our ancestors didn't think of this before." Kasen reached into his coat and brought out the picture, but he didn't turn it around so she would see anything. The reminder was enough. "You're going to let them pick up your scent and know you didn't flee Juneau, and you're going to get them to tell you all about their families, every detail. I don't care if you have to shake your ass or give up your ass. You're going to do it, Shiya, because you are a Keith and because it's the least that Mom deserves."

Chapter Seven

Kotori stretched his arms over his head and stood at the water's edge. The chilly temperature served to cool his anger, but only so much. He kept replaying the incidents that happened in Shiya's suite. What stuck out in his mind most—the part that threatened to send him into a rage— was when that stupid human claimed to be Shiya's fiancé. Breathing deep and stepping farther into the water was the only thing that would keep him from hunting the man and killing him. Kotori glanced down at the wound on his arm, which Birk had stitched. Already it was healing, and if he shifted into his bear form, it would go much faster.

He stared out at the water, his lips compressed, unmoving except his chest as it rose and fell with each heavy breath. Maybe they should have killed her, too, because she had led Joe there and because it was likely the rest would come to hunt him and Birk, maybe even pose a threat to the rest of his family. When he considered Shiya's death, though, he couldn't fathom it. He *wouldn't*. Something inside rose up and insisted on protecting her instead. The emotion angered him, unsettling his thoughts even more than they already were.

He yanked his shirt over his head and tossed it aside. His pants and boxers followed. He'd already removed his boots and socks. Now that he stood naked, he let the wind and cold whip about his body. Goose bumps rose on his skin, but they soon gave way to the change. Silvery white hair sprouted from every follicle, and his skin darkened to the shade natural to the polar bear. His body grew several times its human size, and he dropped forward onto all fours. Curved black claws sprang from his fingertips and from his toes. He raised his nose to the sky and let a roar rip through the air.

He waded out into the water, and his ear canals and nostrils closed just as he dove beneath the surface. With powerful strokes, he swam in the murky, freezing depths. His keen sense of smell told him prey swam nearby. He could pick up the scent up to forty miles, but he chose not to hunt today.

When he came up out of the water, he shook the excess liquid and ice from his fur. He transformed to his human form and stretched his muscles again.

"Feel better now?"

Kotori bent to pick up his jeans before answering Birk. "Not in the least."

His friend grunted. "I've gone over everything a million times. What I thought would happen when we confronted Shiya didn't."

"I still don't know what you hoped to gain. You kept asking her why she slept with us, but isn't it more or less the same as why we did with her? She's hot as hell, and since I lay between her legs, all I can think about is how much more I want. Her flavor, her scent, the way she walks and talks . . ." He shut his eyes and chuffed with the voice of the bear. "Damn it!"

"None of that matters now," Birk grumbled. "She'll leave our little city the second she can arrange a flight out of here, now that she knows her cover's been blown. And that human with her." Birk's nostrils flared, and Kotori figured his friend's rage boiled to the surface as much as his own.

"We could kill him," he suggested.

Birk eyed him in annoyance. "We're not killers, despite what they think of us, Kotori."

"You can't tell me you don't want to claw his throat apart!"

"I didn't say that."

Kotori sat down on the hard-packed ground and drew his feet close. He didn't like putting his feet in his socks and boots wet, but he'd neglected to bring a towel with all the distracting thoughts. Still, he wouldn't have to go far since he had another pair of boots and more socks at the cabin. After the blowup at Shiya's, he and Birk decided to come out to the lands farther north, where the temperatures dropped well below freezing at night, and patches of snow could be found even in summer. They preferred it that way and often shut out civilization to get a few weeks of peace. When Birk couldn't come because of work, Kotori traveled to the spot alone. When he couldn't, his friend enjoyed the solitude.

"If she leaves Juneau?" Kotori asked, staring out at the water.

Birk swore and ran his fingers through his hair. "We've never been this careless. I was a fool not to see how important she became when I talked to her online."

"We always knew when *the one* came along, she would likely belong to us both. Maybe it's just lust. After all, we've been consumed with it before and did some dumbass things."

"When we were boys," Birk said. "I thought we'd matured enough by now."

"Guess not." Kotori stood up and prepared to return to the cabin. His stomach stirred with hunger, and if he wouldn't hunt, then he needed to cook the human way.

"If we get her," Birk said, "her family will come."

"That's what we want, isn't it?"

Birk nodded. "We have to make sure they don't find us just yet." He grinned. "More time to have a little fun, don't you think?"

Kotori grinned, his mood lightening for the first time in two days—the last time he'd seen Shiya. "Now you're talking."

After they'd had lunch and spent the night at their cabin, Kotori rose in anticipation early in the morning. He gathered up his pack and stuffed it full with supplies he'd brought with him, and a few herbs for his grandmother, chief of which was the devil's club. Ever since he told her he would not turn Shiya away, they hadn't spoken much. He knew she would respect him and speak if he insisted, but he wouldn't push. Let her have her space for now. Eventually, he knew she'd come around, and bringing her back the herbs would go a long way to making that happen.

The moment Kotori entered Juneau, he knew Shiya was still around. He took care of a bit of personal business first, and then met with Birk after he'd done his.

"Are we doing this now?" Kotori asked.

"Not yet. Let's get a lay of the land first."

Kotori understood what Birk meant. They wouldn't knowingly butt in on another man's woman, but the animal in both of them felt

Shiya belonged to them, and going against instinct proved difficult. Kotori had learned that the hard way a long time ago.

They traveled to the downtown area in Birk's SUV, Kotori in the passenger seat with the window partway down. He breathed in the crisp air and knew when they grew closer to her. Birk spotted her first, wandering from shop to shop as if she had no specific direction. No bags hung from her arms, and no purse. He studied her face as they drove by, Birk looking for a parking spot. Confusion, worry, and other emotions flitted for dominance over her beautiful features. Did she wonder if they would return for her, or was her concern about failing her family because she hadn't gotten them beneath the hunter's boot, so to speak? Either way, what Kotori desired was to put her over his lap and spank her sexy ass, and then he wanted to fuck her there.

His cock hardened with those types of thoughts, and he ran a hand over his face. Calm, he needed to be calm to confront her. Birk, the more levelheaded of the two of them, would take the lead, and he could feast his eyes on her and listen.

"We need to get her soon," he warned Birk.

"I know, but not here. Too public. If she's afraid . . ." Birk frowned. "I hadn't considered if she doesn't want to be with us."

"We've never had to force a woman."

"No, but then we've never been with a human one either."

"Hm." Kotori had no more patience. He slipped from the vehicle and started walking even while Birk sat double-parked waiting for someone else to pull out of his or her spot. His friend would catch up when he could.

Kotori met Shiya on Shattuck Way. He figured she was just walking at that point with no particular destination in mind. When she stopped at Gold Town and stared into the window at the display, he moved up beside her and leaned on the wall. "You're still here."

She started and looked up at him. He saw the pain in her gaze, but it disappeared quickly, and she forced a smile. "Yes. How are you?"

He ignored the question. "So you have a fiancé, yet you slept with us." Making it sound like a casual question seemed like a crash and burn to him, but she didn't appear to notice. Her frown, complete with pursed lips, was too cute for him to look away. At that moment, he felt more like the Big Bad Wolf than a bear. Would she run if he told her how much he wanted to taste her? A bit of his desire must have shown in his eyes, because he got a sudden whiff of her pungent cream and almost lost it. He imagined her soaking her panties and himself delving for more with his finger or his mouth while she cried out his name.

"I'm not engaged."

Relief flooded Kotori's system. "You say that, but he was pretty intense about it—about *you*."

"Believe what you want to believe. At this point, I don't care." She waved a hand and turned away, but he snaked a hand out to grab her arm. She winced in pain, and he jerked back.

"What happened? I didn't grab you that hard."

Her gaze skittered away from his, and he sensed she was about to lie. After a beat, she appeared to change her mind.

"My brother visited me, acting like a butthead. He's gone now, so it's not a big deal."

Kotori pushed his hands into his pockets to keep from putting his fist through the wall. As a human, she could not understand the seriousness of what she had just told him. "Listen to me closely, Shiya. If he comes near you again, I will deal with him."

"What do you mean 'deal with him'?"

"He has no right to touch you—ever again."

She studied his face. "You're different from the way you were when we went on the tram."

"I'm the same."

"But you're more intense. I don't know how to put my finger on it."

She sighed and turned to walk. He fell into step beside her. How could he tell her he'd always been this way, just short of losing control and reaching out for what he wanted? He smiled at her, had conversation with her, but all the time, he wanted to possess her, to fill her with himself. The night they had sex, it took everything inside him not to do all that he'd fantasized about to her. *She's human*, he reminded himself. He had grown up with his family, a few shifters but not all. Even the ones who couldn't change were strong, so he came to the belief that humans were very fragile. Still, Shiya took him and even liked the way he stretched her to fit his cock. Seeing her face that night had sent him close to the edge. Now she thought he was different, because his desire lurked close to the surface, threatening to spill over.

They ended up at the pub they visited the first night Shiya arrived. Kotori sat on the opposite side of the table from her to keep his hands to himself. He ordered a beer for himself and a hot cocoa for Shiya. They sipped in silence until Birk came. His friend took the seat next to Shiya and ran the back of his hand along her cheek. The move demonstrated possessiveness, and Kotori wished he could be so free to touch without risking so much.

"So why are you two talking to me after what happened?" she asked. "You know who I am, and Joe tried to kill you—" She gasped. "I can't believe I didn't ask about your arm, Kotori. Are you okay?"

"Is a cut worse than being dead?" He didn't know where the bitterness came from and put it down to her mentioning the man they had left in her room with her. Kotori didn't smell the guy's scent on her, so he was sure nothing had happened between them.

At his words, Shiya flinched, and Birk glared at him. "Cool it, Kotori. That's not what we're here for."

Kotori drained his beer and ordered another.

Shiya took a sip from her mug and set it down with care. Her big brown eyes focused first on Birk and then him. "I guess we're all here because there's something between us we haven't finished exploring. Am I right?"

Kotori hadn't begun to get to know her body yet.

"I guess you can put it that way," Birk agreed.

Birk leaned in close to her until his lips came just short of brushing hers. The full, soft lips invited Kotori from across the table. He shifted in his seat, trying to find space in his jeans for his cock.

From what Kotori could figure out since she'd said her brother visited, he wanted results, and he would not accept that Shiya brought him none. That probably also meant they were close—*too* close. His and Birk's idea to get Shiya out of Juneau was a good plan. They would make sure no one followed. The cabin they'd visited the last couple of days wouldn't work for their purposes. The one no one knew about, far north, into the area few humans ventured, would work better.

Relief flooded Shiya's expression, and she smiled. Kotori felt like the sun shined in the restaurant, and he coughed to clear his throat. Birk appeared also to have trouble containing himself. Was she really their . . . No, he couldn't bring himself to admit it, even in his mind.

Shiya laid a hand on Birk's and one on Kotori's. He turned his palm faceup and laced his fingers with hers. He felt the shiver pass along her arm and stroked a thumb over her skin. The warmth there intrigued him, and he breathed in her scent. Next to her, his friend caught it too. Shiya wanted them. She could not fake it if she tried, but she wasn't trying to. Her mission included seducing them. Theirs involved enjoying every inch of her incredible body and then waiting for the others to come so they could destroy the hunters. Shiya would not admit to the truth, and they chose not to enlighten her to the fact that her brother and whoever the rest of the hunters were had underestimated the Alaskan shifters. They would not live to regret it.

"So do we want to use my place?" she offered. "Or one of yours? I think you said you live in the borough, Kotori? No, you said you don't." She frowned.

Birk chuckled. "We'll handle everything. You be ready for us when we come. We won't stay at your suite this time. We don't want to be interrupted."

She ducked her head. "I'm so sorry about that." She glanced at Kotori.

"I'm fine," he told her. "Good as new."

Her eyes widened. "You don't heal that fast, do you?"

Birk stood up, cutting off the conversation. "Why don't we see you back to your room, and you can get ready or rest. We'll pick you up later this evening. Sound good?"

She hesitated, and Kotori almost hoped she would deny her name and pledge to stay with them forever. If she did that, of course, their plans would crumble. He wasn't willing to give them up just yet. Apparently, neither was she.

"That sounds great. I'm sure I'll need a nap with you two. Nine sound good?"

"Sure," Birk agreed, and Kotori nodded. "Have dinner because I don't want to waste a moment eating . . . well . . . depending on what it is."

Shiya blushed, and they left the pub to return to Birk's SUV. Birk dropped Shiya off at her suite, waited until she got inside, and they drove off.

"So we're doing this?" Kotori asked him.

"Yeah, we're doing it. We need to make preparations."

Kotori scratched his chin. Stubble grew already even though he'd shaved that morning. Shiya had noticed when they were out together alone that first time. He wasn't sure if it turned her off. He would shave again before they picked her up because he didn't want to irritate her soft skin.

"I'm wondering how she'll make the trip," Birk said, cutting into his thoughts.

"That's a five-hour hike," he agreed.

Birk drove to the end of the street and turned right. "I need to drop by the hospital. You're coming with me or what?"

"Drop me here. I need to pick up a few items and deliver the herbs to my grandmother. What time are we really picking her up?"

"Six."

"Okay, see you at five thirty."

"Later."

Chapter Eight

Shiya woke in the lap of luxury, or that's how it felt buried beneath mounds of warm blankets. Still half asleep, she stretched and yawned with her eyes closed. Rolling to her side, she became aware of something crackling, and her sluggish mind identified it as a fire in a fireplace. The thought of that lulled her, and she smiled, blinking. The room she lay in wasn't familiar in the least. Where the hell was she, and when did she come here? She sat up and then gasped. The heavy blankets slid down to reveal that she had not a stitch of clothing on.

"What in the hell is going on?"

As she climbed from the bed, she scanned the place—rustic decor, including wooden walls, a slanted roof, and sturdy furniture only a man would choose. There were no pictures, and the curtains hanging from the window did nothing for her in their boring forest-green color. Was this a hunting lodge? She wrapped a sheet around herself and ventured farther on bare feet. The bedroom she left led into a larger room, a combo living room / dining room / kitchen. Off the main area, she spotted another bedroom and a bathroom.

She stood in the center of the floor, trying to remember what happened when she met with Birk and Kotori. They arrived at six rather than nine like they'd said, and she hadn't done more than shower. Once again, they caught her undressed, and she'd made them wait. While she pulled a comb through her hair and pinned it up, Birk had brought her a glass of wine and told her they'd sip it while they waited. She did and . . .

Shiya frowned. "Those bastards!"

She reached up to her hair and found every pin she'd put into it gone. That dang Birk hated her hair being pinned up. She stomped over to the front door, expecting to see a quiet street in Juneau with Roberts Mountain as a backdrop. When she stood in the entry, the sweep of arctic air took her breath away and almost froze her to death with nothing but the sheet as a barrier. Oh, there were mountains, all right, but they were farther away than what she was used to and in several directions. No street appeared anywhere, and snow covered every inch of ground.

Shiya slammed the door and scooted back to the fireside. She slid her feet as close to the heat as possible without burning her toes and hugged her arms around herself. Soon she warmed up, but her temper soared.

A good hour passed before sounds outside the cabin alerted her the men had returned. She'd searched every corner of the small cabin for her clothing and found none, so she'd put on one of the guy's shirts. Her bare legs stuck out of the bottom since no amount of finagling would help their pants to stay up on her.

Birk was the first to walk in, stomping snow from his boots. She stalked over to him and blocked his path. "Where the hell am I, and what did you put in my wine?"

He smiled. "Hello."

"Don't hello me. I want to know what you did. And it looks like we're in the middle of nowhere. How did I even get here?"

"I carried you." Kotori came into the cabin and shut the door behind him. She shifted her glare to him, taking in his words.

"What do you mean you carried me? Are we close to Juneau?"

"No." Kotori pulled the hat off his head, and she noted his wet hair. The man must have wanted to catch his death of cold. He sat down to shed his boots and socks. When he tugged the shirt over his head, she lost track of her thoughts, taking in his bare chest.

"Is that all you have to say?" she demanded when she pulled herself together.

"And where are my clothes?"

Birk scooted up behind her and wrapped his arms around her waist.

Butterflies fluttered in her tummy. He teased her earlobe with the tip of his tongue and sucked it between his lips. She suppressed a moan and forced her eyes to stay open rather than drift closed like they wanted to.

Birk's throaty voice drove her temperature higher. "Why do you need clothes when you look so sexy in this sheet?" He pulled the material away from her breasts to take a peek, but she slapped his hand.

"I'm beginning to think you two kidnapped me."

Birk moved nearer until she felt his hard cock against her back. He ran his hand down over her stomach to cup her sex. "Isn't this what we agreed on? Someplace away from your suite, where we wouldn't be disturbed, so we can get to know each other better?"

"Yes, but I didn't agree to be drugged, damn it!"

Birk grew serious and turned her in his arms. He raised her chin and looked into her eyes. "You're not afraid, are you, Shiya? You realize Kotori and I would never hurt you?"

She considered putting on a show or at the very least demanding to be taken back to civilization immediately and never speaking to them again, but Birk was right. They had decided to enjoy each other without interference.

Inside, she struggled with what Kasen had said to her. She knew she would never allow him or her dad to kill innocent people, and the thought of what happened to her mother warred with her desire to overlook what Birk and Kotori were when she hadn't done so for any other shifter. She couldn't look into these two men's eyes and let them touch her body and then turn around and allow them be killed. However, she also couldn't pretend that they did not have the ability to be instinctive killers if they determined a threat. The cold, hard fact was, that included her. If they thought Shiya would harm them, they would end her life first.

"Fine," she said at last. "I will stay, but I don't like your methods."

"Why, because your people can't track you here?" Kotori said.

She glared at him.

He walked over to her. When he pulled her into his arms, Birk let go, and Kotori kissed her. She was pissed and wanted to deny him, but instead her lips parted to allow his tongue entry.

After some time, he raised his head, and she stood there with slitted eyes, drunk off his kiss. "While we are here, there is no one else. Not your father, not your brother, or any of the men who work for you. You won't have your cell phone, and you will be given clothes to wear." His gaze swept over her form, and she saw appreciation in their dark depths at her bare legs. "While I love you in my shirt, the clothes will fit you because you'll have to be able to go outdoors with us."

She wrinkled her nose. "Outdoors?"

"Yes," Birk answered. He picked up the rest of the instructions. "You will be entirely at our mercy. However, at any time, you can call it quits. No more pleasure. We will take you back to your suite, and you will not see us again."

Shiya said nothing. From their explanation, she got the impression that it was all or nothing. She had to trust them and do what they wanted or go home. When Birk said she wouldn't see them again, she began to think that meant not even on the street. They would disappear, and the Keiths wouldn't find them again.

This was her opportunity. Either she learned enough about Birk and Kotori to satisfy herself that they were not like other shifters, or she would confirm that they were and let her dad kill them without remorse.

Still she hesitated. "You know it's colder than a monkey's grip out there, right?"

Both Birk and Kotori appeared puzzled. She clicked her teeth together to keep from laughing at them wondering how a monkey's grip could be cold.

Birk spoke up first. "We will ensure you're warm."

"But Kotori's hair was wet."

"I went swimming," he explained.

"I'm *not* going in the water!"

Kotori stroked her back and kissed her again. "Don't worry. We wouldn't expect you to. You could not survive it. We won't make you do anything unsafe for humans. We promise you that. What we will do is pleasure your lovely body and bring you to multiple orgasms every day you're with us. We'll do a little experimenting as well."

Intrigued, Shiya bit her lip. The gleam in Kotori's eyes told her he had plans for her she didn't want to miss out on. Even for a little while, she could stay. A few days might be nice, and no one could say she wasn't doing her job.

"I don't see why I can't have my cell phone," was her last argument.

"Your phone is modified to get reception even up here. Your family saw to that." Birk cast her an accusing glare, for which she rolled her eyes in answer. "Our rules and our terms. You can take them or leave them."

"I don't see why you two are making all the rules and I'm making all the concessions." Neither rose to respond to this argument, and Shiya huffed in annoyance. "Fine, I agree."

"To everything?" Birk asked.

She nodded. "Let the games begin."

"First things first." Birk pointed to a huge backpack that appeared to be half her height.

She glanced from it to him. "You're not asking me to lug that over here, are you?"

He grinned. "No, I want you to go and unpack it."

She put her hands on her hips. "Have you brought me up here to be the maid, because I have to tell you, one, kiss my ass, and two, kiss my ass."

Kotori smacked her ass. "All in good time. Go do as he asks."

She decided to humor the two of them for the moment, but if things didn't get interesting real quick, someone was getting an earful. When she unzipped the first section of the bag, she found packaged condoms. No surprise there. The next area contained clothing, but Birk ordered her to bypass those for the next zipper.

"Just how many compartments does this damn thing have?"

The third section caused her to gasp. An assortment of goodies clogged the space, from ropes to ribbons to sex toys. She reached in and pulled out a butt plug. She raised an eyebrow to the guys, but hid her excitement. Next, she pulled out lubricant and oil for heating, in a couple of different scents. The last two items had her confused. The plug made sense, but not the two sizes of dildos.

Kotori responded without her having to ask. "Remember we talked about anal sex."

Oh yeah, she recalled, and his thick cock scared the crap out of her, even for her pussy. She swallowed, imagining it in her ass.

"I want to ease you into it," Kotori said. "The two sizes will help us to take it slow. These two, and then Birk, and then me."

Shiya's emotions shot from fear straight to horny. What Kotori proposed was like getting four cocks, one after another. *Okay, Shiya, calm down, girl.* She thought about it. From what she'd learned about the two of them, Birk loved taking her more from the front, but Kotori had a fetish for anal sex. If she could take him the way he craved her, she might eventually be able to take them both at once. His plan seemed like the best way to go. Now what did they have in mind for the rope?

She curled a length of ribbon through her fingers and ran it over her cheek. "So do I get to tie you guys up with this?"

Birk grinned. He strolled across the room to the couch and sank onto it with easy grace. "Is that what you want?"

She narrowed her eyes at him. "Something tells me you'd never let me do it. You like to be in control."

"That's true, but I also want to give you what you want." He reached his hands over his head, stretching, and causing his shirt to pull over his hard-muscled chest. She wished he'd just take it off like Kotori did, and Birk smiled as if he knew her thoughts. "Is that what you want, Shiya? To have me at your mercy?"

"I might."

"Then by all means . . ." He put his hands together, wrists touching at the sides, and held them out to her. She didn't move. "Well?"

She looked from him to the ribbon and licked her lips. "Are you serious?"

"Definitely."

"And if I wanted to blindfold you?"

"I'm all yours."

Shiya stood up with the ribbon in her hand. She glanced at Kotori, but he said nothing, nor did he try to stop her, so she began tying Birk's hands together. The red silk ribbon slipped over his skin, and for some reason, its delicate beauty compared to his hard roughness turned her on. When the knot was in place, she paused to examine her handiwork. Now what did she do?

"I need a blindfold, Kotori."

Her second lover disappeared from the room and came back with a strip of black cloth. She wondered what he tore it off, but didn't ask. Climbing onto Birk's lap, facing him, she tied the blindfold behind his head and kissed each eye under the mask.

"Can you see?"

"No." He tried nuzzling close to her to kiss her, but she moved out of reach.

"Oh no you don't. You have to earn that."

Shiya rose up on his lap and unbuttoned his pants. She reached inside his boxers and began stroking his thick, hard cock. Birk moaned and raised his hips, but she stopped moving. She stood up in front of him and leaned in so her pussy brushed his face. Birk breathed deep, and she knew he scented her heat. She rubbed closer to him, and he murmured something, sending vibrations through her clit. He tried running his bound hands up her thighs, but she sprang away.

"No touching. Just your mouth."

"Yes, baby. Come here so I can eat you."

She shook her head. Even tied up the man ordered her around.

Kotori stood and walked up behind her. He held her hand as she climbed onto the couch again and stayed close. When she raised her shirt, he kept it from falling again. Shiya leaned in toward Birk's mouth, and as if he sensed her coming, he stuck his tongue out. The first swipe over her clit sent chills racing up and down her spine. She reached in front of her and parted her folds.

"Lick me, Birk." She put a heel up on the back of the couch, and Kotori's strong hold kept her balanced. His small kiss to her ass cheek made her melt, and she reached back to tangle fingers in his hair. In front, Birk snaked his tongue between her folds and slid it upward. Her clit throbbed, and she whimpered. "Yes, like that."

He tried speaking, but she yanked his head to her, forcing his mouth flush against her sex. She put both hands on the back of his head and arched her hips. The slow pump grew faster with the intensity of his eating her cream. She couldn't get enough, and if he concentrated on her clit, she knew she'd come too fast.

"Stick it in me again. I'm so wet, Birk. Lick it up."

He growled, and she watched him strain against the bonds. He wanted his hands free to stroke her thighs, to control how hard she pumped. A few sharp stabs of his tongue into her channel sent her pleasure through the roof.

She bent her knees a little and slid up and down over his mouth. Her juices coated his face, and still he licked with urgency. She cried out, and then it felt so good, she could no longer stand. She was about to get down when Kotori stopped her.

"Let him finish it," he told her. "I will hold you."

"But . . ."

"Stay still. I have you." His strong hands encircled her hips, and she rested her ass against one of his shoulders. He didn't appear to strain at all, but she balanced with a hand on his other shoulder. Birk, realizing she'd moved farther back, followed his nose and his hunger. He leaned forward and claimed her pussy with his mouth. She screamed and spread her legs wider. Birk made greedy noises as he laved her entrance. When her come was gone, he moved to her clit and sucked the small bud into his mouth. She cried out again. When had she lost control of this situation?

Fingers steepled together, Birk ran his hands up one thigh and down the other. He found a way to tease her opening with his thumb while licking her clit. Tremors shook her legs and weakened her to do anything other than feel. She moaned his name and pleaded for more.

Just when she thought it couldn't get better or any more intense, Kotori took the full weight of her body on his forearms and hoisted her legs. Her folds opened, exposing more of her sensitive clit. Birk launched onto it, in sync with his best friend. When the sensations rolling over her were too strong, she tried pushing him back, but he bathed her clit with steady movements.

She squirmed and begged. Her climax reached fever pitch. At last she came, powerful and unyielding, and come flooded her channel.

Kotori flipped her off his shoulder and tossed her onto the couch. He followed her down beside Birk and feasted between her legs. Shiya squirmed beneath Kotori's expert tongue. The aftershocks of mini orgasms zinged up from her core. She turned over, ready to crawl away, but Kotori didn't give up his treat. He grabbed hold of her thighs and pushed his mouth between her legs to capture the last of her come. By the time he was done, she whimpered in a prone position, unable to move.

Kotori rained kisses over her back, along her spine, and down to her cheeks. He massaged her skin and climbed up over her to kiss her lips. She shivered when the cold steel from his belt touched her skin, and he drew back. In seconds, he removed the rest of his clothing. Birk snapped the ribbon from his wrists with no effort at all and stood to undress as well.

She licked her lips, taking in their sexy bodies, and sat up to cop a feel of Kotori's hard thighs and Birk's ripped abs. She leaned in to run her nose along the lines of Birk's contours, breathing his male scent in deep. Her head spun with the desire for him and Kotori building up. So what she'd come already? She needed more.

"Are we using the ropes now?" she asked when she saw Kotori pick them up.

He set the bundle aside. "No, I'm working with your sweet little ass. I can't wait to be able to get inside it, so the sooner the better."

He held the bottle of oil and strode over to her. Her throat dried, and she swallowed, but it didn't help. Her nerves had gone haywire. While she wanted it, she thought of the pain.

Birk laid a hand on her knee and stooped to meet her gaze. "Hey, easy. We won't hurt you, Shiya. You're too important for that."

Important. She wondered if he meant for drawing her family or for being their sexual partner. Something deep inside wanted it to be about her and not her family, but she'd determined to leave speculative thoughts out for now, along with any- and everyone else in the world. Here, in this cabin, only Kotori, Birk, and she existed.

Birk reached down and lifted her into his arms. He carried her through to the bedroom and deposited her on the bed. Shiya thrilled at his and Kotori's strength to just toss her body around like she weighed nothing.

Kotori climbed onto the bed with his toys on one side of her, and Birk moved in on the other. She lay back, resting her hands on their thighs. Tiny silky hairs on both men's legs teased her palms, and she ventured farther to nudge their ball sacs and their tight cocks. Her pussy clenched the second she wrapped her fingers around their rods, but both stilled her hands.

"If you start that, I'm going to finish it here and now," Birk promised her.

"Don't make threats . . ." She grinned at him and raised one knee. Both of their gazes locked on her pussy. She couldn't believe the power she had over two of the sexiest men—shifters—she had ever seen. Rolling to her stomach, she hiked her ass in the air and glanced from one to the other to gauge their reactions. Birk didn't hesitate. He stuck a finger into his mouth and brought it out moist to massage her hole. She gasped and moaned. Okay, it wouldn't do to forget the same game she played, they played better—and they could double-team her.

Kotori squeezed oil into his palm and rubbed his hands together. She thought he was going to use it on her hole, but Birk turned her over to her back, and Kotori began rubbing her legs with the oil. Birk grabbed the bottle and squeezed some into his hands. With the same procedure, he worked on Shiya's other side. Soon their hands were everywhere, dipping between her legs and grazing her clit, but slipping away before she could get too excited.

They massaged every muscle from her feet to her neck, and then flipped her to work the back. One set of hands teased her ass cheek, and the other followed suit. She arched as both Birk's and Kotori's fingertips kept nudging her anus. After a while, she couldn't take it anymore and begged for release. Birk made a *tsk* sound and waggled his finger at her.

"Not yet. You will get to come again when I say, not before."

She pouted. "How did this get turned around? I was supposed to order you to do what I want."

Birk ran his fingers down between her cheeks and pressed against her sensitive opening. She moaned and shut her eyes. His low chuckle sounded in her ear, and she shivered. "How long did you think that would last? Just what do you think I am, little flower?"

Her eyelids snapped up, and she stared at him. His eyes had gone jet-black, and little white showed around the sides. She parted her lips and took in shallow breaths.

"I'm going to eat you and eat you until I can't take any more, and then I will take more still." He raised her leg and smacked her ass. He rubbed and pinched her skin and smacked again. Her pussy grew moist, and she chewed her bottom lip. Birk's intensity scared her, but it turned her on too. She realized that both men hid a lot of their true nature, and only now had it come to the surface. They didn't even try to hide their lust. She just hoped she could take it.

Kotori set aside the oil and selected another bottle from his stash. He squeezed the liquid onto his fingertips and worked it around for a few moments. She wondered what the difference was between the two. Birk supplied the answer.

"The oil could cause a condom to break, but this lubricant won't."

"Works great with this too." Kotori held up the butt plug, evil intent in his gaze.

She buried her face in the pillow beneath her head, but raised her ass a little. Kotori began working the lubricant onto her hole and pushed slickened fingers inside her. She wiggled her hips, moaning at the pleasure. So far, there was no pain, and she welcomed more.

Kotori wrapped an arm under her to lift her hips higher as he worked the plug in and out of her ass. He pushed it in and wiggled it around in a circle, driving her crazy. She cried out his name and scratched at the sheets, but Kotori didn't leave her pleasure stagnant. He quickly moved to the smallest of the dildos and popped the head past her barrier. She gasped at the feeling of fullness. All the energy drained from her body as her walls began to stretch around the tool. Kotori eased it farther in, and she struggled to catch her breath. A slight ache started up, and she winced. Birk's hand shot out to Kotori's wrist.

"Stop, damn it! You're hurting her," he growled.

Kotori froze. "Shiya?"

The concern in his voice surprised her, and also went a long way to helping her calm down. She willed her muscles to relax and waited until the twinge went away. "Do it, Kotori."

He took his time guiding the dildo in and pulling it out. He rotated it in a circle, sending tremors throughout Shiya's body. Her core spasmed in bliss, and she reached under herself to rub her clit. Birk caught her at it and took her hand away. He replaced hers with his own and pinched her swollen bud.

She keened through an unexpected orgasm with Kotori thrusting the dildo into her ass at a rapid speed.

When the sensations passed, she pushed Kotori's hand away and rolled to her side to rest. Her chest rose and fell with each pant, and her heart raced.

"I need a break," she pleaded.

Kotori sat back on his heels, and she glanced down at his rock-solid cock. She'd come two or three times, and they hadn't once. She didn't have to look over her shoulder at Birk to know his state was similar to Kotori's. Pushing up to a sitting position, she reached for Kotori and encircled his neck when he drew her close. He raised her up and brought her down on his tight cock, and only after they pounded together and she was screaming her head off enjoying it did she realize he forgot to put on a condom.

Kotori pushed her back on the bed and flattened his big body on top of her. He pounded so hard, her hips grew sore, but she didn't care. She pushed her heels against his ass and arched up to meet his thrust. A growl erupted from his throat and rumbled in her chest. He gave another mighty push, threatening to render her unconscious. His seed spilled deep inside of her, and before she could draw another breath, Birk replaced his friend. He reared back on his haunches and raised her heels in the air. His long, smooth cock slipped between her folds, and she gasped. Birk ground deep and slow, but with as much violence as his partner. He pulled out, turned her facedown, and climbed over her body. As she peered over her shoulder, she watched him spoon her ass and felt his cock penetrate her pussy. Birk laced his fingers with hers and buried his mouth against the side of her neck. He filled her with his cock again and again, murmured her name in her ear, and told her how tight and good her pussy felt.

Shiya lay still as he claimed her, and a subtle orgasm rocked her to her core.

Seconds after, Birk grunted, "I'm coming!"

Neither of them moved until long after he found his release, and Shiya's eyes drifted closed as she lost track of time and the world.

Chapter Nine

Snow crunched beneath Shiya's booted feet as she stepped outside of the cabin. A few feet ahead of her, Kotori strode with the ease of a man who had done this a million times, and Birk brought up the rear. She stumbled in the spots with deep snow and uneven ground, amazed at the terrain up here as opposed to Juneau. Sure, the weather there would turn soon enough, but it still seemed interesting, probably more so because of the guys than anything else.

After some time of walking, Shiya's leg muscles began to ache, but just when they did, a stretch of water appeared just ahead. She gasped and stopped moving. Polar bears dotted the landscape, some nosing along in the ice and snow and some slipping into the water to search, no doubt, for seals. Her heartbeat kicked up a few notches. Birk stopped behind her and cocooned her in his arms. His and Kotori's coats weren't as thick as hers. They had dressed her like a

Christmas goose with all the layers, but she hadn't complained.

"Don't be afraid," Birk said somewhere above her head.

She tilted her head back to look at him. "Are they shifters?"

"No."

She wondered if he lied to protect the others, but she detected no hesitance as he spoke. "They're regular bears who spend a great deal of time in this area and farther north. This is a safe spot for them—and for us."

She didn't need to ask him what he meant by "safe spot." From the interference of humans, probably. "Won't they pick up my scent and be annoyed or whatever?"

"You're with us. They know we're different than what they are, but they respect us as we do them. They will not touch what we've claimed as our own."

Claimed as their own? Temporarily, I guess. Thinking that this would end in a few days lowered her mood, but she shook off the feeling. On impulse, Shiya broke from Birk's hold and bent down to form a snowball. She chucked it at the back of Kotori's head and hit it spot on. That's what came of being Kasen's sister.

Kotori rubbed the back of his head and spun slowly on his heel. The look of confusion made her crack up, and then he was on her.

She screamed and ran, but his long legs ate up the ground between them. He caught her around the waist and did some kind of twist in the air. Shiya landed on top of him in the snow. She wiggled to get free, but his embrace was a vise.

Kotori picked up a handful of snow and held as if he would smash it in her face. "You deserve this. Take it like a woman."

"No, no," she shrieked, laughing.

She sat up on his lap, pulling at the arm he held her to him with. Birk charged up and smacked the snow from Kotori's hand. "You're not hitting her with that, you idiot."

Shiya took advantage of Kotori's distraction and got free. She rolled to her feet and started running again. The wind bit at her skin and was so cold, it seemed to freeze her lungs, but it liberated her too. To let go and just enjoy herself felt incredible. Her mukluk boots crunched the snow beneath her feet, and her toes stayed warm. The coat Birk provided her with did the trick to keep her cozy, but didn't weigh her down too much as she ran. Behind her, the guys argued, Kotori insisting he wouldn't do anything to hurt Shiya and Birk accusing him of not liking to lose.

Shiya stopped running and bent over holding her side as she laughed at them. Stupid men, they wasted time slinging around testosterone when they could have been pursuing her. Now that she thought of it, though, Birk and Kotori never seriously argued with each other. They seemed to exist in harmony, and she considered whether it was because they understood each other's place in the friendship and respected it. They never seemed to compete to pleasure her or got jealous of the other. *If they were human, would it be different between the three of us?*

"Shiya!"

The anguish in Birk's tone sent a chill of fear crawling up her back. She looked at him, but he stared past her, and so did Kotori. Shiya went still, almost scared to turn around. From the corner of her eye, she noticed the polar bears walking farther down the shoreline, as if they'd all agreed to vacate the area as one. Some backed away as if they were giving the right of way to something. She licked her lips and swallowed, bringing to mind all she knew about the beautiful animals.

Polar bears were the largest land carnivores. They were the biggest bears, the male growing up to fifteen hundred pounds. While they easily outweighed the brown and black bears, they tended to move out of the vicinity of another type of bear rather than confront it. Shiya's knees grew weak, and before she could move a step, the chuffing sound told her she'd guessed right. A bear was behind her.

A tremor started throughout her body, and she looked toward Birk and Kotori. Their clothes lay in a pile on the snow, and two polar bears charged toward her. This was the first time she'd seen them in their animal forms, and she wished she'd focused on them earlier so she could watch the change.

They were both bigger than all the other bears, and their coats were thick and silvery white. Long black claws cut into the snow and ice as they ran, and their growls of anger sent chills down her back.

Shiya spun around and screamed when the black bear rose up on hind legs. The beast stood closer to her than she thought. While bears were heavy and bulkily built, she knew they were more agile than they appeared, and not even the fastest human could outrun them.

Although she knew she should keep still, fear had her stumbling backward. The black bear growled and swiped a powerful paw toward her. All she could see was those claws ripping her face apart. Seconds before it hit, a locomotive smashed into the bear, and it and the polar bear rolled in a tangled heap over the snow. A white paw swung and then a black one. They growled and chomped at each other, and Shiya's heart hammered so hard in her chest it hurt.

She struggled to her feet, still shaking. The second polar bear walked in front of her, blocking her from the fight, but he kept his eyes on the two warring bears. She wondered which was which—who guarded her, and who fought. Either way, she worried about him getting hurt, or worse, killed.

Without thinking, Shiya curled her fingers into the hair of the polar bear in front of her and leaned against his big body. All at once, she realized which of the two men fought on her behalf. An image of Kotori zipping past her to throw Joe against the wall came to mind. Kotori, the one scarcely containing his emotions, the more dangerous of the two. Now that she compared the polar bears, she saw that the one fighting was built bigger.

She inched along Birk's expanse and wrapped her arms around his neck. His small ears twitched, and he chuffed in annoyance, watching Kotori fight.

Something told her he wanted to jump into it, but he didn't want to leave Shiya alone in case this bear wasn't by himself.

"Please, Birk, don't let him get hurt," she begged. She had no idea if he understood English in this state. "This is my fault. I shouldn't be out here. I'm sorry."

Tears sprang to her eyes when, over Birk's head, she saw blood staining the pristine white of Kotori's fur. "No, no! Birk, help him."

The bear growled, but he ignored her. Kotori reared up on his hind legs and came down hard on his enemy. The black bear dropped to the snow and didn't move. She thought he'd killed it, but when Kotori took a few steps back and then growled, it struggled to its feet, turned, and walked off. Shiya waited until the black bear was far off before she ran around Birk and scrambled over to Kotori.

"You're hurt." She touched the spot where the blood stained his coat, but she couldn't get past all the hair to see the cut. He nosed her hands away.

"Don't be grumpy. You have to be treated. Let's go back to the cabin."

She stood up and went to gather their clothing. Both Birk and Kotori stayed in bear form, and she knew it was to be sure there were no other threats.

When they arrived at the cabin, both men shifted. Shiya stood in awe of the way the white hair seemed to melt off their bodies while their bulk decreased as if by magic. One minute they were gigantic beasts with elongated bodies, and the next they were men—very *naked* men. She hurried them into the cabin and slammed the door. After tossing aside their clothing, she rushed to try getting the fire stoked in the fireplace, but Birk nudged her aside.

"I'll take care of it." He nodded toward Kotori.

Shiya dug through their supplies and wasn't surprised to find a first aid kit. She knelt on the couch beside Kotori. The slash lay on his side, but it wasn't as bad as she'd thought. "This is my fault. If I weren't—"

"Stop," Kotori interrupted. "This isn't your fault. It's a way of life for us. Sometimes there will be fights. It's not a big deal."

She frowned. Knowing all the facts about the animals didn't help her to understand their nature. "He shouldn't have been there."

Kotori shrugged. He didn't even wince when she touched the iodine-soaked cotton ball to his skin. "I am more impressed that you weren't afraid of us."

"Well, you were protecting me, weren't you?" She kept her eyes on his wound, embarrassed for some reason.

He stroked her cheek. "I'm glad you weren't afraid."

"She also knew us apart," Birk announced, and Shiya heard the pleasure in his tone. He sat down behind her, his thigh brushing her ass. Neither man had bothered to put on clothes. This was another natural state with them, she realized.

When she finished treating Kotori's wound, she placed gauze over it, and secured it in place with medical tape. She touched the scars on his neck, a stir of emotion making her throat hurt. "Was this a bear too?"

He stiffened. "No." Kotori's gaze flicked to Birk and then back to her. "Another fight, a wolf. I tried making a claim for someone already taken."

Shiya frowned. Kotori left out a lot of details, but she thought she could piece it together. He didn't want to say, but the wolf, she guessed, was another shifter. "You went after his girlfriend, and he had a problem with it?"

Kotori's brows went up, and Birk laughed. "That's our baby, very astute."

"Under normal circumstances, he wouldn't have been a problem for me, but he laid in wait and sprung out on me with his pack. Very nearly took my voice."

Shiya shivered at the violence he'd suffered and marveled at the calm with which he shared it, again as if it were no big deal. From his hesitance, she knew it was much more than that. Kotori blamed himself for what had happened. "It wasn't your fault, you know."

He pierced her with an angry stare, but she blinked at him, not intimidated.

He grumbled, "If I had not let my emotions get the better of me, I wouldn't have tried to take another man's woman. We respect the claiming of mates above all else no matter what species of shifter we are."

"We're all weak at some point," she assured him.

He made no response.

"No rules apply when we're fighting for our mate," Birk added, and then he grinned. "But we got them back later, ran the entire pack out of town. Haven't seen them since."

Shiya shook her head. "I feel like I've learned a lot about you today."

Birk touched the top of her head, and she twisted around to face him. He pulled her onto his lap, and she nuzzled beneath his chin. "There's always a reason for an attack, Shiya. Remember that."

Did he say it in reference to her mother's attack? She didn't know, but resentment rose inside her. Birk had no right to comment. He couldn't know the facts or the devastation she felt about how her mother suffered before she died, as well as the rest of them having lost her.

She climbed off his lap and went to the kitchen area. After all the excitement, she was starving. Birk walked in behind her and took the eggs from her hands that she'd just removed from the refrigerator. She said nothing to him, but he went about making the three of them something to eat.

Kotori went to his room, and when she accepted there was nothing for her to do to help Birk, she followed Kotori. In the room, he lay on his bed, an arm thrown across his eyes. She watched him from the doorway.

"Did you love her?" she asked.

He didn't start at her voice, and she remembered she couldn't sneak up on them because of their sensitive hearing and their strong sense of smell.

"No. She played me for a fool. She wanted to push him to make her his mate. She was not alpha material, so I doubt it worked out in the end."

"I thought you said you had to respect her as his mate, but now you're saying she wasn't?"

"He claimed her as his by marking her. He did not complete it with a bite and a declaration before his pack. When he does that, it would mean she's an alpha like him. He let his dick lead him regarding her. No different than I did, I guess. She wasn't an alpha."

The jealousy that stirred in Shiya's belly made her grit her teeth. What did this woman look like that she caused Kotori to forget his principles to have her? She supposed she should just drop it. The woman was old news, a long while ago, from the appearance of his scar. Kotori's concern seemed to be more about his decisions than about caring for the woman.

Shiya decided not to bother with examining her own feelings. She liked being with Birk and Kotori. She definitely enjoyed the sex, and she would leave it at that. After crossing the room, she sat on the bed and removed her boots.

Kotori raised his arm to allow her to settle in next to him and lay her head on his chest. They waited in silence for Birk to bring the food.

When her second lover came in holding two laden trays, she shook her head at his strength and sat up. Kotori slid to the top of the bed and hoisted her between his legs. She leaned on his chest while Birk placed the tray beside them.

"Wow, I don't think I can eat even a quarter of what you have here," she said. Bacon, eggs, sausage, ham, rolls, and bread enough to feed an army crowded the plates. "Are you sure you're not wasting food, Birk?"

He winked. "When we shift, it must eat up a lot of energy because Kotori and I are starving beyond reason. A typical polar bear can eat forty pounds of food a day. This isn't that much."

"Damn near it."

They ate in silence, Shiya having drawn her knees up to rest her plate in front of her. Birk eyed her half-empty plate and frowned. "Aren't you going to finish that bacon?" She shook her head, and he leaned over to nab the last few pieces with his fork.

Shiya rolled her eyes. "How could your mom afford to feed you? Come to think of it, I know you have a sister that you don't have much to do with, but you never told me why."

Birk finished up the last of his food, piled her plate on his, and set them both on one of the trays. He moved the trays to the floor and then pulled her knees down so he could rest his head on her thighs.

"My sister didn't inherit the shifter gene, but it was the one thing she wanted more than anything else. A long time ago, she left Alaska, and I haven't heard from her since. When my parents passed within a month of each other, she didn't attend either funeral, and I had no number to contact her. She made her choice, and I accept that."

Birk's words sounded determined, yet she heard the hurt and loneliness. He loved family and wished he had more of one. She knew that much from talking to him before she flew up here.

"I'm sorry your relationship isn't better. Maybe someday you'll find a wife, and she'll birth you lots of babies."

All three of them fell silent at such a ridiculous dream coming from her. She felt like an idiot. Kotori's question surprised her.

"Would you like to have children someday?"

"Of course. I'm just like most other women." Despite the family she had been born into, she longed for someone to love her unconditionally and the chance to have his children. "I always dreamed of having four. My mother used to tell me to wait until I felt the pain of just one to be sure of that number. As a little girl, I thought she was just teasing me because I was her fourth, and she used to tell me often I was one of four perfect gifts."

Kotori's arms encircled her, but she didn't need comforting. The tears she'd cried nonstop for her mother were all dried up, and while it had hurt beyond belief, the past could not be changed.

"Shiya," Birk said, and she looked up at him. The pain in his eyes startled her. He hurt for her mother's loss on her behalf. Her heart constricted, and she leaned down to kiss his lips. He caught her when she tried to pull away. "Tell me everything."

"I . . ."

He waited. She looked from him to Kotori and turned away. They didn't push, but she felt the support from both of them. They wanted to know, and she desired to tell them what happened, even if it hurt. After all, Kotori had shared his painful past.

"We . . . *they*—my parents—were on an assignment. I always admired the way my father allowed my mother to take the same type of jobs my sisters take. I was the only oddball who stayed behind the computer."

Kotori made a sound of surprise, and she looked up to see it in his eyes.

"This was your first time trying to seduce a shifter?"

She winced. "I guess that's kind of a compliment since you couldn't tell." She glared at Birk, feeling afresh the sting at his previous words about her and her sisters whoring with their kind. "I've never been out of my home office, except to sit in the back when there was an interview. That was the closest I'd come to a shifter."

"An interview?" Birk said.

She ignored his question. "Contrary to what you think, not one of us has slept with a shifter. I was the first."

"Don't be so proud of it," Birk snarked, annoyed.

She flicked her gaze over him. "What, you think you're all that?"

His hand snaked out to her breast and covered it. In an instant, her nipple hardened, and he poised a thumb above it as if he would strum the tiny peak. She forced her gaze away from him, trying for an appearance of being unaffected. The low chuckle told her she fooled herself and no one else.

"Stop teasing her, Birk, and let her finish her story." Kotori didn't fool anyone either, because she felt his cock twitch and stiffen behind her ass.

"The job was supposed to be routine. My mom would enter the bar and sit near the jaguar shifter. She would make contact and get him to talking. All she had to do in this case was to draw him out, but something went wrong. Another man outed her as a Keith in the bar. I don't know how he knew or what connection he had. My dad and my brother dealt with it, but they refused to share the details. The next thing any of us knew was we found my mother dead in a motel room. She'd been tortured and then left to die. That was five years ago, and we have been reminded every day how cruel shifters are, how vicious."

Birk sat up and touched her cheek. She turned her face away, but he made her look at him. "What did I tell you, Shiya?"

She glared at him.

"I said there's a reason for everything we do. *Everything.*"

Kotori added his thoughts. "Yes, we are part animal, but we are part human too. We have reasoning where our counterparts do not. That can be challenging going up against instinct. As we've pointed out earlier, the greatest reason for a man to forget his human side is when someone touches his mate or his family. You don't want to hurt a man's mate and leave him alive."

The way Kotori said it sent a dead chill over her being. She thought about it. Her father and brother kept a lot of things from the women, even though they said they were all in this together. The interviews almost never included the women, and the only reason she'd sat in on one for a short period of time was because her dad hadn't noticed. When he did, she was shown the door.

Now she'd heard straight from her brother that they wanted to kill Kotori's entire family. Birk's sister might be safe since even he had no idea where she lived, but what about Kotori's grandmother? The old woman hated her, but she didn't deserve to die, and neither did his parents or siblings. She gasped at the way she was thinking. When she stepped off the plane, she'd thought she was firm in her beliefs about the rightness of what her family was doing, but really, she'd already begun to doubt. That started when she began chatting online with Birk.

Shiya climbed off the bed and walked over to the window. She pulled the curtain back and stared out at the snow with the beautiful mountains in the distance. If she could, she would never leave this cabin. She'd keep Birk and Kotori close, but who would protect the others? What if her family found out about the rest?

"Kotori." She spun around to face him. "Is your grandmother safe? I mean, she can't be used to . . ."

He rose and came to her, tugging her into his arms. His big hand cupped her neck, and she tilted her head back to receive his hungry kiss.

Oh no, I want to be with him and Birk forever, but they're not offering that, and how can I? They can't trust me. I'm a Keith.

Kotori raised his head, and the gentleness in his eyes robbed her of the ability to speak. She had expected lust or any number of emotions close to the surface in his readiness to take her. What looked like love scared the hell out of her. She closed her eyes, deciding it was wishful thinking.

Besides, she'd just shared with them about her mother's death. If anything, she should feel hate, shouldn't she? Rage? That's what Kasen wanted her to experience when he showed her the picture. Yet, she knew she could never hate these two men. Something about Birk and Kotori had gotten deep inside of her, and she didn't know whether they were unique or just like every other shifter out there in the world. What she did believe was that they were not vicious or evil.

"My people are fine," Kotori assured her. "I made arrangements for them before Birk and I brought you here."

Her eyes widened, and she dug her nails into his arms without meaning to. "Do you plan to kill me?"

Birk strode over and stood behind her. He stroked her hips and pressed in tight to her ass. She went up to her bare toes and stuck her ass out to him. Birk moaned. He raised his hands to her breasts and gave them a firm squeeze. "We couldn't kill you without cutting out something vital to our existence."

Totally unsexy declaration of love, but she would take it. Shiya dipped her head and hid a grin. There was no telling how a relationship between the three of them could work out long term, but right now was not the time to figure it out.

"I need to work off my breakfast."

Kotori growled low in his throat. "Is that right?"

"Yes." She looked up at him and tilted her head a little in challenge. "You know how I can do that?"

"Definitely!"

Chapter Ten

Birk reached from behind her and unbuttoned her pants. He had them around her ankles in seconds. Even as he yanked her panties down with one hand, his other one cupped her pussy. Her jaw went slack, and she covered Birk's hand with hers.

"Yes, that feels so good, Birk. I want to come so bad."

"Easy, baby. You will. You want to please Kotori?"

"Mm," she murmured.

Birk raised her legs and pulled them apart. He took her full weight on his forearms and held her in readiness for Kotori. Her second lover undid his pants and shoved them low over his hips. Kotori's hunger was such that he didn't wait to get fully undressed. He stepped forward, grasped her hips, and thrust hard into her pussy. Shiya cried out in both pain and ecstasy. She took all of Kotori's fat cock and arched her hips to drive him deeper. They pounded together, withdrew, and ground in again. Birk stood like a brick wall. No matter how hard Kotori pushed, he provided a staying power to keep her in place while his partner slaked his lust.

"Mine now," Birk said in a clipped tone, and he tossed Shiya into Kotori's arms.

Kotori pulled out of her wetness only long enough for Birk to moisten his fingers in her dripping come. Birk dampened her ass, thrusting first one finger in and then another. He worked them in and out until she whimpered, dropping her forehead to Kotori's shoulder.

When her anus muscles loosened, Kotori raised her a bit higher so Birk could guide his cock into her pussy. She cried out his name, but he didn't stay there long. He wet his cock with her juices, and then switched to her rear entrance. He took it slow, easing in one inch at a time. Shiya shuddered with the powerful sensations. She collapsed against Kotori's chest, unable to do anything, but he held her up until Birk seated his cock to the hilt. Then Kotori thrust his dick into her once again.

For the first time, two men filled her. The squeeze overwhelmed her mental faculties. She didn't move or make a sound other than to moan just a little.

Birk's cheek touched hers. "Okay, baby? It's not too much?"

"No." Her voice came out a whisper.

She hung between the two men as they began moving in and out of her body. As one, they took her, their thrusts going from gentle to rough. Kotori was the wilder of the two. Because her pussy had taken his sexual beating, and his best friend's, many rounds before, he didn't hesitate to pound into her, driving his hips forward. Because he wasn't as long as Birk, he didn't have to worry about how deep he could go. He let loose, raising her thighs higher and grinding until she thought she'd lose her mind.

In the same way, Birk broke in her ass. She had the feeling by the time he was done, there would never be a need for a dildo. His stiff shaft would always be at the ready. His fingers bit into her hips as he thrust into her hole.

She whimpered when he matched Kotori's movements. They ground into her from the front and back like a well-oiled machine, each knowing his part.

As if they'd rehearsed the move, Kotori stopped pumping and pulled out of her while Birk took her weight. Kotori dropped to his knees and sucked her clit into his mouth.

She screamed and squirmed. Her hand shot out to push him. "Wait, Kotori, too much, too much!"

He refused to back off. He laved her little bud with wild abandon and stuck his tongue into her pussy. While he licked at her juices, his thumb worked her clit. Birk continued to pump into her ass. She pleaded, but the men refused to listen. When her orgasm slammed into her body, it seemed to take over her entire being. The zings of pleasure shot from her core, down to her toes, and even made her light-headed. Not once did either man stop. Kotori kept eating her pussy as if he would never stop.

"Oh, baby, you feel so good," Birk murmured behind her. "There's no way we can stop. I'm never going to stop! This pretty ass is mine, and I will have it as long as I want."

Shiya gasped at the possessiveness in Birk's words. She didn't think he could fuck her any faster or harder, but she was wrong. His intensity increased until she almost bounced off his erection. At the same time, Kotori didn't let up from the front. She felt the beginnings of another climax and could do nothing but allow them to do what they wanted. Somehow she felt the same.

She belonged to them, and satisfying what they wanted was, at that moment, her entire purpose for existence.

Birk found her lips and covered her mouth. He stuck out his tongue, and she sucked it, her eyes shut and tears on her cheeks. She knew when he came because he jerked behind her. He grabbed one of her inner thighs and squeezed. The other arm was slung across her midsection, fingers curving around her waist to drive her tighter to him. An orgasm pierced her core.

Kotori, knowing her body, shifted from her clit to her opening in time to eat the cream with deep, guttural moans. Birk emptied his load inside of her, and then Kotori had her, carrying her across the room to the bed.

He deposited her on the mattress. "On your knees, honey."

She did as he commanded, facing away from him. She knew this was it.

Kotori would stretch her beyond reason with his big cock. She bit her lip, but Birk moved around the bed to capture her face in gentle hands.

"It will be fine. Your incredible body is made for him. Let your mate inside you, Shiya."

My mate . . . two of them.

To be sure she took him with no unnecessary friction, Kotori used lubricant on her entrance and on his cock. She thought she might freak out if she looked, so she kept her gaze on Birk's face as he sat in front of her. The easy confidence in his expression went a long way to settling the wild tattoo of her heart, but when Kotori pressed the tip of his cock into her ass, she fell into Birk's arms.

"Hold on, Kotori. Let her get used to it." Birk scooted closer and held her against his chest, while she arched her back and Kotori lowered his hips so they wouldn't lose the right angle. She panted, trying to calm down. Her dark lover stroked her thighs, raising goose bumps on her skin. He flattened his length along her back, fueling her desire. Even holding still, the fullness stole her energy, but it felt good too, bringing her close to a faint.

"I'll stop if you want me to," he whispered, but she heard his desperate hunger. Kotori had been waiting for this, to lay claim to her ass in the way that he'd pounded into her pussy. Just the thought of it excited her.

Almost sitting on Kotori's lap with her legs spread, she guided his hand to her pussy, and he pinched her clit. She sank back slowly onto his cock. A cry was torn from her throat. She licked her lips and lost control of the speed with which she sank. Birk caught her around the waist. His gaze locked with hers, and then he lowered her down. Inch by inch of Kotori's cock sank into her ass. The painful stretch didn't overwhelm her, but it existed all the same.

Kotori held still and allowed Birk to take the lead in helping her adjust to his thickness.

Shiya dropped her head back and closed her eyes. "It hurts."

"It won't for long, baby." Birk kissed her lips. "I promise."

She reached full penetration, and Kotori growled his pleasure. His nails were suddenly claws, and he ripped the sheets apart. She knew he did it in an effort to keep from slamming in and out of her ass. Birk pushed her back until she rested on Kotori's chest.

"Hold your cock, Kotori," Birk told him.

Kotori did so, and Birk raised her hips until his cock slid all the way out of her, and then he pushed her back down onto it. She whimpered. Birk repeated the movements, raising her off Kotori's shaft and then lowering her onto it again. Over and over, he steered their coming together until her body expanded and allowed her lover full access without fighting. At some point, pain turned to intense pleasure, and Birk gave over control to Kotori.

Kotori's arms locked around her. He pushed his hips up, grinding his cock into her sore hole. His hot breath warmed her ear as he pressed his mouth to the sensitive spot behind her ear. "Do you know how long I've waited to take you like this?"

She heard the roughness in his tone, almost angry. His embrace tightened, and he caught her nipple between his thumb and forefinger. Shiya's jaw went slack. She gasped for breath with each thrust.

"You belong to me now, and I'm not going to give you up—to anyone."

"K-Kotori."

He sank deep inside her and held there. Birk cupped her pussy and pushed two fingers between her folds. The heel of his palm rubbed her swollen bud.

They were going to force her to come again. She didn't think she could stand it, and yet, each man seemed beyond letting her decide how far he went. Not that she blamed them. The stimulation drove her to the edge of sanity, but she'd never experienced such pleasure.

"Do you like my dick in your ass?" Kotori demanded.

"Y-Yes, oh yes."

"And do you want me to come in you?"

"Yes!"

"How badly? Tell me how bad you want it."

She licked her lips again, not sure of the words. Kotori gave her one pump and stopped moving. She felt a shudder pass through him. He was on the edge, and even if she said nothing, he would lose it soon. She wanted to do whatever he asked.

"I want it, Kotori. I want it so bad. I can't get enough of you. I love your big cock. Please, give me all of it."

"Good girl," Birk said and turned her chin so he could kiss her.

While he devoured her mouth, Kotori began moving again. He thumped his broad erection up her ass at lightning speed. Her breasts bounced, and he rolled her nipple between his fingers. She shouted into Birk's mouth, and then Kotori went still. Warmth stole over her insides, and Birk dropped a hand between her legs. He rubbed her clit in a circular motion until she shook. Her climax came on the heels of Kotori's release, and she gave over to the bliss of it until it faded away.

Birk drew her into his arms and carried her to the bathroom. He waited until Kotori filled the tub with warm sudsy water, and she wondered, not for the first time, how they had running water out here. Maybe something they'd rigged themselves or had contractors out to do.

Kotori tested the temperature and then stepped inside to sit down. He held his arms up for Shiya, and Birk handed her over. Soon she lay back against Kotori's chest, watching with slitted eyes as Birk washed his amazing body.

She followed with her gaze his hand as it soaped and trailed down over his belly to his cock. Inches away, on his feet, he tempted her as he bathed his shaft. Already, it stood at attention. He placed the soap in her hands, and she lathered them to wash him. She started at his cock's head and moved to his balls, being careful not to hurt the sensitive sac. Hungry to touch every part of him, she moved to his muscular thighs and down to his calves. She reached around to his ass and washed there. Her arms weren't long enough to reach beyond his abs, but Birk took the soap and set it aside. When he knelt down in the water, Kotori elevated her legs and parted them. Birk wasted no time pushing his cock into her pussy. With his rough entrance, water sloshed over the side of the tub. No one cared. Birk kissed her lips as he thrust into her.

"Oh, baby, your pussy drives me insane." He put a wet hand to her hair and gave a gentle tug that made her put her head back. He claimed her throat, kissing and licking along its length. "I'm going to have to fuck you all day and all night."

"Do whatever you have to," she managed to say between shallow breaths.

"Give me some of that," Kotori demanded, and he turned her head to ravage her mouth with his. She parted her lips and took his tongue between them. Shiya moaned, tasting him. Her heart swelled because she now knew how much she loved both of these men. Kotori didn't allow her to think too much on her emotions when his growls became desperate. He tore his mouth from hers. "Not enough!"

Birk eased back and raised her up. As soon as he had room, Kotori aimed his cock to her ass and pushed in. Birk lowered her onto Kotori and shoved his cock back inside her. Taking it from both ends, Shiya cried out in bliss. Her mind shut down as they pumped deep into her pussy and her ass. They thrust hard, withdrew, and thundered forward again. She collapsed on Kotori's chest, but an orgasm began to build, shaking her to her core.

She clutched Birk's shoulders, at first pushing him away and then pulling him closer. "Too much, too much! No, don't stop. I need it. I'm going to come."

The words had no sooner left her mouth before she fell apart, her climax taking full control. Watching her come seemed to take the guys' lust to a whole new level because their roars of pleasure turned animalistic. They pumped harder and faster. Darkness clouded in around Shiya, and for the first time in her life, she fainted from being oversexed.

When Shiya opened her eyes, she lay in bed, warm blankets thrown over her naked body. She rolled over and moaned. Every muscle resisted movement, and she whimpered.

"I'm so sorry, baby." Birk's hand came down on her head, and he stroked her cheek. "I hate myself for being too rough with you. I should have known it couldn't work with a human."

She gasped and sprang up. Her body screamed for mercy, but she ignored it.

"How can you say that? It was good, wasn't it?"

Kotori walked into the room holding a glass of juice and something in his hand. She realized both men were dressed. Worry niggled at her gut. Pain choked her at the words Birk spoke, which were obviously a rejection.

"Here, baby, take these." Kotori handed her two pills. She recognized the pain meds and wished it were three. Two had never worked on a regular headache. Grateful anyway, she took them and swallowed the meds with the juice.

Kotori sat down on the side of the bed. Birk had drawn up a chair to watch her sleep. He leaned forward now and made her lie back. She didn't fight him because her arms shook with the weight of holding herself upright. They'd worn her out, that was for sure, but it was only because she needed time to get used to their lovemaking.

"I just need time. I'll adjust." Neither man responded, and she bit her lip. She would not beg to be with them. No one had claimed this would be long term. "Hey, don't worry about it. It was fun, and we had a great time, didn't we? If nothing else, I will walk away from this with a greater respect for your kind. I can't, in good conscience, hand you over to my family. I'll . . . I'll find some excuse, and that will be all there is to it."

She thought of how angry Kasen had gotten when she'd called it quits before. Well, he could get the hell over it. She would not be bullied to betray Birk and Kotori. Whether it was right to love them or not, she did, and she would not stand by while someone killed them. Maybe going back was the best way to protect them. She could control what information her family gained about the shifters and know that they weren't targeting Alaska anymore.

Grogginess settled over her, and she yawned. "Just let me get a little more rest, and I'll be ready to head back down to Juneau with you. Like I said, it was amazing. I hope you two enjoyed yourselves even though I wasn't able to keep up." She peered through her lashes at them, and the misery clouding their handsome faces shocked her.

"There is no pleasure outside of you, Shiya," Birk said.

"Ditto." Kotori's answer was more a snap, filled with anger and impatience.

She reached her hand out to him, and he took it, brought it to his nose, and breathed deep. Birk slipped from the chair to the bed and drew her onto his lap. He buried his nose in her neck.

They act like they love me. Why don't they say it? Why don't they let me stay?

Her heart shattered, and she didn't mean to do it, but she started to cry. Birk crushed her in his arms, and Kotori drew the covers around her. For a long time, they stayed in that position, until she drifted off to sleep.

Once again Shiya woke from a long sleep. This time, a noise jarred her awake. Her mouth felt like cotton, and her muscles hurt no less. She rubbed her eyes to try to get the sleep out of them, and the pounding came again. She sat up and scanned the room to find she was back in her suite, in bed. Her heart plummeted.

"I know you're in there, Shiya. Open this damn door!"

Kasen. She slid from the bed and looked around for clothes. An outfit lay neatly folded on the chair with her cell phone on top. The guys. She noticed they'd powered off her phone, probably to allow her to get some rest. She smiled, her eyes growing wet. She would not cry, no matter what. Her decision had been made, and now was as good a time as any to let Kasen know that.

She pulled on panties, jeans, a bra, and a long-sleeved shirt. "Hold on, Kasen," she shouted and darted into the bathroom to brush her teeth. When she thought she looked presentable enough, including boots on her feet, she went to answer the door. Making the man wait this long, he'd probably be in a sour mood, but that couldn't be helped.

Shiya swung the door open and gasped. "Shae!"

Her sister darted into the room and scooped Shiya into a tight hug. "Hey, girl."

Shiya grabbed her hand and dragged her over to the couch to sit down. "I thought you were in Maine. What in the world are you doing all the way out here?"

Shae rolled her eyes. "Drama queen over here made me come. He said you needed my help."

Kasen stalked around the room, checking closets as if he thought she hid shifters in them. His black mood radiated off of him until Shiya wanted to scream at him to get out. She turned back to her sister, who traveled so much, she didn't get to see her as often as she liked. They talked on the phone daily, though, and when Shae had time in the evenings, they Skyped.

"Sweetie, where were you the last few days?" Shae asked her.

Shiya looked at Kasen, who'd gone still, and then back at her sister. "I . . . I was doing my job."

"Yeah, fucking those things," Kasen snapped.

Shae glared at him. "Get out."

"Excuse me?" Kasen stood over the two of them, his brows dropping low and his lips tightening. A nerve jumped in his jaw. "Maybe I need to remind you, Shae, that you—"

"Maybe I need to remind *you* that I don't answer to you, and that bullying shit you do with Shiya won't fly with me. I'll beat you down and send you home to your wife. Don't play with me, Kasen, because I'm not the one. Now let me talk to my sister alone!"

He stabbed a finger toward Shae. "You're pushing it, girl, pushing it hard. You better watch the way you talk to me."

She stared him down, and Kasen spun on his heel and left the suite, slamming the door behind him.

Shiya let out the breath she didn't realize she'd held. "Damn, you're good. Can you really beat him?"

Shae laughed. "Girl, no, he's vicious in a fight, but you can't let him bully you. Kasen won't go but so far. He knows Dad would cut his balls off if he hurt one of us. So aside from that, what's going on, Shiya? Kasen told me something I didn't like to hear. I especially didn't like getting it from him and not you."

Shiya couldn't meet her sister's eyes. "Kasen should get his mouth off my business."

"It's not just your business, is it? I mean, you're out here on a job. You begged Dad to let you do it. I knew it would be hard, but I was confident you could pull it off."

"And now you're not?" Shiya rose, getting her back up.

Shae grabbed her wrist and tugged her down. "Don't get your panties in a wad, Miss Missy. Just tell me straight. Did you have sex with those monsters?"

"They're not monsters!"

"Shiya."

She sighed and dropped her head into her hands. "Shae, they're not. They're men who happen to be able to shape-shift into polar bears."

"Do you hear yourself?"

Shiya looked up. "Haven't you ever been tempted?"

Shae laughed. "Of course! Are you kidding me? They're all sexy as hell. It's like the gene guarantees they will have bodies a woman wants to lick day and night. My job has me kissing one of them every now and then, and let me tell you, not one does it wrong. But at the end of the day, I know what they are. I *know* their kind tortured and killed our mother."

"So all humankind should be punished—no *killed*—because of the murderers."

"Not the same."

"How?" Shiya faced her sister down and waited for Shae to give evidence that would change her mind or destroy the love she felt for Birk and Kotori. "Did you know Dad and Kasen agreed to kill their entire families, even people who are not shifters?"

Shae gasped. "You're lying."

"No, I'm not. Kasen told me himself. I thought he was just saying that to get to me, but he said Dad thought it was a great idea so we don't have to revisit places after a couple generations when a new shifter is born. What about the innocents? What about the children? We will be no better than what we're trying to eradicate from the earth."

"We'd be murderers ourselves," Shae agreed. "This is the first I'm hearing about this, but you bet your ass I'm going to bring it up in the family meeting next week. I'll put a stop to it, and I'll get Sakura to help."

Shiya blew out a breath, relieved. "Good."

Her sister laid a hand on Shiya's knee. "Sweetie, that doesn't change the fact that those two guys . . . What were their names?"

"Birk and Kotori."

Her sister gaped, and Shiya frowned.

"What?"

"You love them. I heard it in your voice. You actually love them—*both*!"

Shiya stood and rushed to the balcony door as if she had some urgent business there. When she swung open the door, cold air swept in, clearing her mind and calming her down. She closed it after several minutes and faced her sister. If she could convince Shae of her seriousness, then the rest of the family would come easier. Not because Shae was hard, but because she loved her the most.

"I'm not turning them over," she said. "Yes, I love them. Whether you think it's wrong or not, I do. I won't let Dad and Kasen kill Birk and Kotori."

"Do they love you?"

Shiya gritted her teeth. "This isn't about whether they love me."

"So they used your body and then threw you away."

"That's not how it is, Shae. You don't know them like I do."

"You said that about Joe in the beginning."

Her sister might as well have stabbed her in the heart. Shiya balled her hands into fists at her sides. "I'm not giving them up. In fact . . ." She heaved a deep breath and squared her shoulders. "I'm leaving the family."

The front door crashed against the wall, and both Shiya and Shae jumped. Shiya's mouth went dry seeing her brother standing there, and something told her he'd heard her declaration. His nostrils flared, eyes slitted, and lips drawn back from his teeth. He didn't know it, but he looked just like one of the animals he hated so much.

"Is that you how feel, Shiya?" He advanced a step into the room, and it took all of her willpower not to retreat. She stood her ground and nodded. He moved closer. "You're going to throw away the family who raised you, loved you, put food on your table, and made sure you never once had to go out into the world and get some menial job as some idiot's secretary? No, you had everything you needed from the day you were born. Now you get a taste of a creature, and you want to throw it away. That's what you're saying to me?"

She put her hands on her hips. "I think I was talking to my sister, and don't act like I was laying around all that time. I went to school and got my degree in computer science. I was an integral part of building the network that feeds the family information from all over the world regarding shifters, so don't even try to belittle me like I'm just some dumb woman waiting for the menfolk to take care of me."

He held up his hands. "Oh no, don't let me insult the computer princess. She might run and tell Daddy." Kasen snapped his fingers, and five men shuffled into the suite and surrounded Shiya.

"What is this, Kasen?" Shae demanded, standing.

Kasen glared at her, but flicked his gaze back to Shiya. "This is me handling things *my* way."

Shae stepped forward, but one of the men grabbed her arm. She had his thumb in a pinch that would render a regular man useless and have him on his knees at her mercy in seconds. Kasen's guy countered the move and had Shae by the back of the neck. She elbowed him in the solar plexus, but he took the hit and blocked more. Over and over, they fought until another of the men joined the first, and they restrained Shae. Shiya saw the fury in her sister's face. There would be hell to pay making her look like a fool.

"Stay out of this, Shae," Kasen told her. "Shiya's going to lure those two guys to me, and then I will deal with them and their families."

Shiya crossed her arms. "I'm not helping you do a damn thing."

She didn't see the slap coming. One minute she stood on her feet, and the next she landed on her ass with her cheek stinging. She leaped up to go after Kasen, but two men held her back by her arms. Kasen stood over her.

"You're going to learn your place, girl."

"And you're going to learn what it means to put your hands on me."

His brows rose, and he laughed along with his boys. "Look at the little princess. She thinks she can beat me."

Shiya took them all in, especially her brother. Her anger, bitterness, and hurt stood above what she felt for him at that moment. "Not *me*."

Kasen's smile froze when he realized whom she meant, but then he forced a smile. "Yeah, okay. Get her out of here. The sooner I'm back home, the better. I'm missing my baby."

Shiya shuffled ahead of the men holding her with Shae in the back shouting for Kasen to leave her alone. Shiya went along for now. She didn't know if what Kasen had planned would work, but she would not be the cause of Birk and Kotori falling into his trap. She needed to escape, and then she would leave Juneau. If she was gone, maybe they would be okay, and so would their people. She had no idea where she would go, and like Kasen said, she'd never had a reason to get a regular job. Well, she wasn't lazy, and she knew her stuff. Someone would hire her.

Never seeing Shae again would hurt, but this was the best choice.

Outside, Kasen shoved her into an SUV, and two of his men climbed in behind her. They secured her hands behind her, and Kasen snapped on plasticuffs.

Shiya winced. "Ouch, you dumbass. That's too tight."

Her brother grinned at her, unrepentant.

"Quiet, you traitor," one of his men snapped.

She didn't know his name, not interacting much with Kasen's men, but she saw the disgust in his eyes. She tried wiggling her wrists to gain a bit more comfort, but it was impossible. Even she knew a person needed to be trained to avoid cutting off blood flow with this type of cuffs. Kasen made sure to train his men in every area of their jobs. She wondered if the cuff would hold a shifter and if they'd been obtained just for her.

Her brother walked around to the driver seat, but he didn't get in. He held the door for one of his men, and when the guy was settled, Kasen thumped the doorframe. "Get her to the location we set up. I'll meet you there. I'm expecting this to be wrapped up in time for dinner."

"You got it, boss."

Not long after, Shiya watched Juneau fade into the distance through the rearview mirror.

Chapter Eleven

Birk slammed a fist on his desk, and the wood splintered in every direction. The sides collapsed. The top snapped in half and caved to the floor. Papers, pens, and other paraphernalia he'd had on top sank into a pile. None of it mattered. Not the fact that he'd just bought this particular piece of furniture, or the explosive noise he'd made with its destruction.

He and Kotori had gone against everything they'd planned from the moment they met Shiya in person. They intended to win her heart and draw her family in. They were the ones ensnared, falling in love with her and claiming her as their mate. Kotori declared she would never come before family, but he'd left his people's side to be with Shiya at their cabin while hers had the run of Juneau. When the time came for them to follow through and hold Shiya to lead the other Keiths into a trap, they'd returned her to her suite and backed off. Now this!

A banging started on his office door, and his receptionist called out, "Dr. Rider, are you okay? What was that noise? Birk?"

He ignored the woman, his focus on Kotori. His best friend's eyes were all black, and his canine teeth hung past his lips. Birk knew Kotori held on to rationality by a thread, because Birk felt the same. "Are you sure about this?"

"I'm sure. I tracked her partway out of Juneau. She's not alone. A half dozen others are with her."

"She could have joined them voluntarily." Birk struggled to keep his head on straight. He didn't want to jump to conclusions, but when Kotori charged into his office and claimed Shiya had been taken, he had flown into a rage before using his head.

Kotori growled, his voice thick as if he forgot how to form words. "Are you coming or not?"

Birk stood up. "First we check her suite. Then we track her. If someone does have her, they will die at my hands."

They left the office without explanation to his staff and jumped into his SUV. All the way to Shiya's place, Birk thought over the situation. If Shiya's own family had her, why would they bother? They had to know where to find him and Kotori. They weren't in hiding. Kotori had sent his grandmother to the mountains where many of them lived anyway, and Birk had no one in Alaska. So why didn't the Keiths just come? Hell, they could have picked him up at the vet hospital, and Kotori at his offices, with some semblance of an excuse.

Well, it didn't matter why. What mattered was getting Shiya back.

"We shouldn't have left her," Kotori complained. "She's ours, and we should have kept her at the cabin."

"Contrary to what we want, we have to think about Shiya's happiness. She's not strong enough to be our mate, and we couldn't hold her prisoner forever." He squeezed the steering wheel beneath his grip and felt the materials giving way. He forced himself to calm down.

"Where she is, I go." Kotori's simple logic attested to his giving over to his animal side.

"Can you adjust to San Diego?"

"I can."

Birk sighed and soon pulled up to the private entrance to her suite. He hadn't set a foot outside yet before he picked up the scent of several men—and a woman. He took the steps two at a time and checked the door. The knob twisted in his hand without hesitance, and he walked in. Two people stood inside the small living room, guns in hand. Birk narrowed his eyes at them.

The man he recognized as Shiya's ex-boyfriend. Behind him, Kotori growled on seeing the human they hated most.

The woman looked so much like Shiya, Birk's chest constricted in pain. She smelled similar as well, but he easily picked out the difference. He kept his face expressionless, but his friend had no such control. He sensed Kotori coiling for attack, and Birk held up his hand to hold him off—for now.

"Where is she?" he demanded.

The woman raised her chin. He caught no glimpse of fear in her eyes and smelled none either. He had to give her credit for that. This must be Shiya's sister. He didn't recall her name and didn't care to. All he wanted to know was where they'd taken his mate.

"You have three seconds to answer me before you die."

The woman waved her gun. "I guess you don't see this weapon, huh? Don't come in here threatening me. I've dealt with your kind before, and I've put them down more times than I can count. As far as I'm concerned, you're nothing but animals that look like people."

Kotori sprang forward, but Birk caught him just in time. He felt like his arms would be torn from the sockets keeping a grip on Kotori, but he managed it. The woman went on.

"However, my sister seems to care about you, and I love her more than anyone on this planet. My brother's wrong for kidnapping her, and I want her back, so I'm happy to send you into his trap. As long as Shiya's okay. But if you get her hurt, if you cause even a scratch to mar her skin, I will pump your ass so full of bullets, you will beg me to die."

"Where?" Birk snapped.

The man, who hadn't said anything, pulled a sheet of paper from his pocket and tossed it onto the floor. "There. We have a temporary compound set up. That's where Shiya is."

Birk snatched up the sheet and saw that a map had been printed on it. He stuffed it in his coat pocket and pushed Kotori toward the door. "Let's go."

Kotori strained against him at first, but gave in. He performed a U-turn in his vehicle and, amid screeching tires, tore off down the street. He had a general idea of where to find Shiya and was glad of the map. They could track her, but knowing exactly where to go cut time. *Hold on, baby. We're coming for you.*

The trip would take several hours, but Birk intended to floor it all the way, even if parts of the road made it unsafe. They had taken Shiya far away from civilization to cover their activities.

"The map," Kotori said, and Birk handed it over. His partner studied it and then handed it back. "I'm getting help."

Birk stiffened. "Do you want to drag your family into this?"

"Won't you do everything for her?"

"Of course." Birk would give his life for Shiya, but he had no one else to protect. He considered it now and knew that if he did, Shiya would come first. His animal side saw his mate as being above all else. Part of the reason he hadn't ripped those humans apart back at Shiya's place for being a part of her kidnapping was because the woman admitted to loving Shiya more than anyone. He saw in her face that she didn't agree with her family's tactics. The rest would not be spared.

"You're right. We don't know how many there are. Don't take too long. I don't want her to suffer a minute longer than she has to."

Kotori nodded, and Birk pulled to the side of the road to let him out. His friend shifted into his bear form and took off running. Birk continued on.

Three hours later, he pulled his car to the side of the road. The rest of the way would have to be on foot. He removed his clothes and left them in the SUV. Then he shifted and headed into the trees. Snow covered much of the ground out here, and his claws and wide, flat paws allowed him to cut through it with ease. Scents not natural to nature tickled his nose. He picked up the smell of humans, a lot of them—and Shiya.

Shiya rolled over on the floor, wincing in pain. Her wrists had swollen and gone numb. Since they dropped her in this joke of a cabin that had nothing on Birk and Kotori's place, no one had come back to check on her. She'd called out, but nobody answered. Every now and then, she picked up voices, men snapping orders and other conversations. The cabin she occupied was one of just a handful. Tents occupied other spots, and she didn't think they planned on staying out here long. Just enough to slaughter an entire family. She needed to get out before Birk and Kotori came.

Working her bound hands to her butt, she wiggled to get her hips through the loop her arms made. Tendons in her arms grew taut, and she paused to catch a breath. Sweat beaded on her forehead, and she hadn't even started yet. After what felt like an eternity, she managed to get her hands down to her knees, and she rolled to her back and sat up. Very slowly, she pulled her knees up to her chest. The only thing she was thankful for at this point was that someone had taken her boots and left her in her socks. She figured they did it to keep her from running out in the snow, but then someone had locked the cabin door from the outside anyway.

She lay on her back and slid her hands down her calves as far as she could, then worked one foot into her palm and through. Her muscles strained and ached. She took a break, panting and moaning. When she managed to get the other leg through, she stood up. What little rest she'd gotten after the marathon of sex with Birk and Kotori had been sapped with this experience.

Voices outside the cabin made her run behind the door. A key sounded in the lock, and the latch gave. She brought her clutched hands down on the back of his head. Her blow didn't knock the man unconscious, but it was enough to land him flat on his face. Shiya kicked the door closed and dropped on her knees in the middle of the man's back.

He groaned in pain. "You bitch."

"Right back at you," she snapped and kneed him hard behind the neck.

Before he could regain his faculties, she jerked his shirt up and grabbed the knife most of Kasen's men carried in scabbards on their back.

The hunter's knife cut through the plasticuffs, and she was free. She ignored the painful surge of blood to her hands and wrists and grabbed Kasen's man by his hair, putting the knife up to his throat.

"If you don't want to get buried out here, you will help me, and keep your mouth shut."

He laughed.

"What's so damn funny?"

He flipped her onto her back and landed on top of her, an arm across her throat. The knife fell from her hand and clunked onto the floor. The bastard shoved it away. "Okay, should we try this again?"

She opened her mouth to say something, but a growl cut her off. The door exploded inward, smashing against the wall. A polar bear stood in the opening, seeming so out of place yet so right where he should be. His baleful gaze bowled from her to the man atop her, and Shiya could only imagine what he thought. She shoved the idiot.

"Get off of me before he kills you."

Kotori lunged at him, but he shoulder-rolled away and snatched his knife from the floor. His crouch looked good, but Shiya knew it would mean nothing. Kotori was in a rage. She sensed it, blown away by the connection.

"Kotori, it's fine. He didn't hurt me. Calm down."

"Don't go near him. He'll kill you!"

Shiya glared at her attacker. "Just be quiet." She stepped in front of Kotori, cutting him off from his prey. "Kotori!" She held her hands up, which turned out to be a mistake.

Her lover focused on the bruises around her wrists where the cuffs had been.

Kotori shifted into his human form and barreled past Shiya. He disarmed Kasen's man as if he were no more than a child and had him several feet off the floor by his neck. He slammed him into the wall and squeezed his throat.

Shiya had a flashback to Joe and rushed over to grab Kotori's arm.

"Stop, Kotori. Let him go," she pleaded.

"You're the one who put those bruises on her?" Kotori demanded, as if he hadn't heard her. Another slam on the wall brought a stain of blood. Shiya's stomach somersaulted.

"He didn't do it," she shouted.

Kotori dropped the man to the floor. Shiya thought she heard a bone snapping when he hit. When he didn't move, she bent to check his pulse. Her heart thundered out of control. Kotori had already killed him.

"Who?"

She swallowed and looked up at her lover.

"Who?" he repeated. He reached down and pulled her to her feet, but his touch was nothing like what he'd done to Kasen's man. Kotori's grasp on her arm remained gentle. She wondered at how he could go from strangling a man to handling her with care. Her hands shook, and her knees seemed about to give at any second, but she didn't fear Kotori. What she did fear was telling him it was Kasen who put the cuffs on. Her brother was all kinds of a bastard, but she couldn't let Kotori kill him.

"It doesn't matter. It wasn't intentional."

Kotori narrowed his eyes and raised her chin. She shivered at the darkness she saw there. "Anyone who hurts you does not get to live."

Staring up at him, all of a sudden, she knew the truth about what had happened to her mother. One of them, her mother, or her dad, maybe Kasen, had killed the shifter's mate. The wolf that attacked Kotori had been defending his rights to kill the man who had touched his mate. Kotori had only seen her bruises. If for some reason she'd been killed . . . The shifters weren't fully animal, but they weren't fully human either. They lived by their own rules, and she understood why that would terrify humans who knew of their existence.

How would she distract him from insisting she tell him? More growls erupted outside the cabin, along with the clink of steel on steel. Kotori hadn't come alone. He shifted and started out of the cabin, and she picked up the knife to follow. The makeshift compound was in an uproar. Polar bears attacked men in several areas. Men in animal skin clothing and mukluk boots held small curved blades as they fought Kasen's men. Their darker skin and long black hair pegged them as Tlingit, Kotori's people.

The scent of blood permeated the air, and it stained the snow in too many spots. Shiya scanned them for Birk. This was her fault. If she'd never slept with them, never asked to get out into the field . . .

When her feet began to freeze, she looked down and winced, remembering her boots had been taken away. At another cabin, she heard her brother's cry and ran in through the open door. Birk and Kasen faced off. Her brother's right hand hung at an awkward angle, but he'd switched his weapon to the left. A gun lay discarded, and she figured Birk had disarmed him earlier.

"Kasen, give up," she demanded. "If you and your people leave Alaska, we can end this fighting."

Her brother sneered. "They all deserve to be killed. You saw them out there, didn't you? There are more shifters here than your two lovers, and every one of those men are carriers. I can guarantee you that. Besides, they cut down too many of my men. I can't let that slide."

"You started this!" She took a step closer to her brother, but Birk reached out and snatched her back. In one fluid motion, he whipped her around him and thrust her in Kotori's direction. Kotori held her close to his side, and she couldn't make him let go no matter how hard she struggled.

"And I'm going to finish it." Kasen feinted left and went right to drive his knife into Birk's side. Birk blocked the move and sent Kasen flying backward. Her brother smacked into the side of a table and doubled over. He spit out blood and dragged a hand over his mouth.

Shiya searched her mind for a way to stop this. "If you don't back off, he's going to kill you. They'll kill all of you. I'm willing to bet you've never come against this many shifters and carriers at once. You're out of your element here, Kasen. Kotori's family are used to the climate, and they don't interact much with those on the outside."

Her brother sneered again. "Meaning they're wilder than the animals we've come across before. They deserve to be wiped off this planet."

Kotori moved up to Birk's side. Where he'd calmed down some after finding her, she saw his rage resurface. She had to end this, or they would bury her brother just as they did her mother.

"If you don't stop, I'm going to wipe out every piece of information you have on the shifters, every contact, every lead."

Kasen swore. "That can be gotten back."

"Ten years' worth? In how long?"

He seemed to debate over it. Her threat didn't hold much water. All Kasen needed to do was contact her dad or someone else at their headquarters and get an IT person to change the access. In seconds, they could lock her out of the system and back everything up.

"Kasen!"

Shiya jumped, and all of them turned toward the new voice in the doorway. She couldn't believe her dad stood there, as calm as if he'd been out taking an evening stroll. His angry gaze locked on Kasen.

"Please explain to me why you have my daughter in the midst of all this fighting."

"Daddy, I'm fine." She tried not to draw his focus on her feet.

"Dad, I—" Kasen began.

"Outside! I want a full report!" Her father spun on his heel, and it was as if both sides agreed to back off for now. Shiya noted from the doorway that all fighting in and outside of the cabin halted. Polar bears melted into the trees, camouflaged by the white snow. Kasen rushed to the edge of the cleared area, frustration obvious in the set of his shoulders and his clenched fists.

"Dad, you know they're shifters, right?" Kasen demanded.

Her dad ignored him and crossed his arms over his chest. Shiya noted how fast Kasen calmed down. No one disrespected her father and got away with it—even her brother.

Shiya began to step out of the cabin, but Birk blocked her path. "Kotori, she needs boots."

Her lover disappeared and returned in seconds with a pair. She wondered whom he beat to take them, but didn't ask questions. Her feet were freezing. Kotori stripped her wet socks off, and held her up while she stuck her feet into the warm boots. Birk waited close by, alert to anyone trying to hurt her. Her heart warmed at seeing them there, but so easily they could have been killed. All around lay injured men, and a couple of Kotori's people picked up their fallen and melted into the scenery.

"We're going, Shiya," Birk said. "I have the feeling your father won't allow your brother to go too far again when it comes to you."

Her stomach dropped. She felt a sob rise in her throat, but swallowed it. The hesitance in Birk's expression made her wonder what he wasn't saying. "Yes, I'm safe. My dad's never been a fan of using us girls. Birk, what are you not telling me?"

He scanned the area. Several of Kasen's men were close, but not in hearing distance. They stood at alert as if they suspected Birk and Kotori would take her. She resented the thought since her brother had started this mess. Birk eyed the men and turned toward the trees. He found his route blocked. Now she knew her dad coming hadn't put an end to the fighting. He'd stopped her being used as the pawn. As far as he was concerned, Birk and Kotori were still on his list. Had anyone told him about her relationship with them? They must have, or he would wonder why she would work as bait in the first place.

Kotori held his hands to the sides, claws forming from his nails. Each one slowly turned black, and he growled low and threatening. Something told her Birk wouldn't stop him if he attacked her family.

She swung to face her father and brother and raised her voice. "Dad, please, just let them go."

Her dad held out his hand to her, standing several feet away. All she had to do was step away from her lovers and over to her dad, but to do so meant turning her back on them. With Shiya so close, her dad wouldn't give the order to shoot Birk and Kotori. She knew how he worked. Yet, she also knew, out there in the trees, even though she couldn't see them, Kotori's people weren't far. They had a standoff, and it depended on her decision.

She looked up at Birk. "You don't want me long term, right? You think I'm weak because I'm human?"

"I don't think you're weak." He touched her cheek, and she heard her brother swear.

Birk didn't spare him a glance. He smiled at her. "I should kiss you thoroughly right here, but it might be too much for them."

"Birk."

"Beautiful Shiya." He sighed, and she thought she saw pain in his eyes. "Kotori killed several men today."

She gasped. The man in the cabin with her wasn't the first.

"If he feels you're threatened, I can't make him back off. Do you understand the kind of man he is?"

She nodded.

"He won't hesitate if it's your dad or your brother. He won't even hesitate if it's your precious sister. Had she stood in the way today . . ."

Her throat dried, and she swallowed, trying to find moisture where there was none. They'd been to her suite, where she and Kasen had left Shae. "My sister—"

"She's fine."

"Th-Then we can't be together," she concluded.

"You're from a family of hunters. Unless they back off, which I think they won't now that they know there are others like us here, we're at an impasse. They kill us, or we kill them. If we kill them, you will never forgive us."

"If they kill you, I won't forgive them either," she insisted.

Birk went on. "Your dad's going to call you to his side, and to keep you safe, we will allow it."

She frowned.

He ran a thumb over her bottom lip. "Damn it, I want to taste that mouth once more. Go to him."

"But they'll—"

"*Go.*"

No! I'm not going to let this happen. I can't.

"Tell me one thing, Birk." She turned to Kotori, whose glittering dark eyes barely reflected reason. Even though he hadn't shifted into the bear, he appeared to be all animal. "Kotori."

He looked at her, and she didn't see recognition in his gaze, but she trusted he knew who she was.

"I want to know how you two feel about me. I want to know if I wasn't a Keith, and if my family had nothing to do with us, what would you do?"

Birk leaned toward her, and his breath warmed her ear. He whispered, "I would move heaven and earth to be with you forever."

Tears sprang to her eyes and fell down her cheeks. She peered at Kotori, and at first, she thought he wouldn't answer or that he didn't understand her words.

"I love you."

The three words stole her own rationality, and she knew what she had to do.

Chapter Twelve

Shiya took a tumble into the snow for the millionth time. She couldn't believe she'd just taken off running like she did, with both sides on her tail. Birk and Kotori could shift and catch her, but she noticed they stayed behind the humans just enough to be out of sight. She had no doubt they were back there—or hell, ahead of her—somewhere. Several of her father's men dogged her heels. When one caught her arm, she went down on purpose and took him with her. A punch to the throat or a knee to the groin got her free.

She had to keep moving. If she didn't, Kotori would attack. She couldn't let the death of another man be on her conscience, but she wasn't willing to give up her lovers either.

She wasn't fool enough to think she could run back to civilization, but if she could get enough distance between her and her father's people, Birk would come and get her. Then she would ask him to take her somewhere she could execute the second part of her plan.

When her lungs burned and a stitch had started in her side, she began to think this whole situation was a bust. Her eyes blurred, and she blinked them several times to clear her vision. A shadow to her right and just ahead brought her to a stop, and she fought to hold her breath so she could hear something other than herself. The effort proved to be too much. She blew out a noisy breath and took a stance, her fists raised and legs planted firm, one leg forward so she could throw a kick.

In every direction, there was nothing, just trees and more trees. Out here, the snow was deeper, and even the boots didn't keep her feet warm. She needed socks. No, she needed a warm fire, some cocoa, and a blanket.

A hand came down on her shoulder. She grabbed the wrist, flipped the hand off, and spun around to throw a punch. Kotori caught her fist in a huge palm, engulfing it with little effort. Curved dark nails touched her skin where he held her, but didn't cut her. When he let go, she threw herself into his arms.

"Birk," she mumbled against his chest.

"I'm here."

She looked around and found her other lover. Just as she thought, they'd circled around and gotten ahead of her.

"You caused quite a stir back there," Birk told her, amusement in his eyes.

"I had to do something."

"Kotori and I could have taken care of it."

She moved out of Kotori's arms and put her hands on her hips. "Yeah, like leaving me. That was an unacceptable solution. Now, if you don't mind, I'm freezing my ass off out here. Can you take me back to Juneau?"

Birk frowned. He scanned the distance past her and sniffed. "They're close. Honey, I don't think they'll let you go so easily. Your dad may have already called ahead to have someone waiting at your suite. Maybe your sister and that other person."

Shiya almost laughed at the disgust in his tone when referring to Joe. "Don't worry. I'm not going back there, but I need civilization just for a short while. I need access to a computer, and then I'll go anywhere we need to, to be safe—*together*."

"You're determined."

"I've never been so sure. I think we Keiths have been blind for a long time, and there's nothing I can do to make up for all the damage we've caused, all the pain and suffering. I threatened my brother with wiping out everything, but I don't think he believed me. I'm hoping he didn't, or that he's been so distracted he didn't call it in. Their network is about to disappear permanently."

The trek to Birk's car felt like it took forever with her being worn out. She resisted being carried, and Birk and Kotori shifted into their bear forms to stay warmer. They flanked her on both sides, small ears perked up on their heads to listen out for the enemy. By the time she climbed into the SUV, she didn't feel like arguing against Birk's suggestion that she curl up on the backseat. She slept all the way to town—or what she'd assumed would be Juneau but wasn't.

She sat up and rubbed her eyes, yawning. The surroundings were still mountainous, full of trees and snow, but several buildings dotted the landscape, with plenty of space between them so one occupant wouldn't feel like their neighbor crowded them. The cabins were all of the quality Birk's and Kotori's cabin had been when she spent several days with them alone. Behind the cabins, some ways off, was a body of water, and polar bears dotted the shoreline.

"Where are we?"

Her answer came when she spotted Kotori's grandmother heading their way. So this was where his people lived when away from Juneau. She could never forget the old woman's disapproving face, but this time, she didn't appear so annoyed when she drew up to Shiya as she stepped from the vehicle.

"You've decided," the old woman said.

Shiya raised her brows. "I'm sorry?"

"Come," the woman snapped. "Devil's club juice will help frostbite."

Shiya tossed Birk an amused, if doubtful look. "Seriously?"

He chuckled.

Kotori, who seemed calmer now, spoke in the Tlingit language to his grandmother and repeated it in English for Shiya's benefit. "She has to take care of some business, and then she will submit to your treatment."

His grandmother appeared to accept his explanation, and Shiya followed Birk and Kotori to one of the cabins. Once inside, she marveled at the equipment—two computers with massive monitors, printers, and other peripherals.

"Damn, what do you have going on out here?" she mused. "And can you even get an Internet signal?"

"Satellite," Birk answered and hooked a thumb in Kotori's direction. "He may look like a muscle head, but he manages a lot of his operations from here. He has a manager for day-to-day tasks and oversees from a distance."

She whistled. "Of course, he's not much of a city man."

Kotori snatched her into his arms as if he would punish her for her criticism, but he tipped her chin up and kissed her roughly. Shiya parted her lips, inviting his tongue into her mouth, and she moaned, pressing closer to him. Birk came up behind and spooned her ass. Her pussy clenched in excitement.

Birk reached around to stroke it, but she covered his hand and broke away from the two of them.

"I'm not getting anything done if you two don't stop." She dragged a hand over her mouth, but missed Kotori's lips. Her gaze met Birk's when she turned. His obvious desire heated her skin, and she had to fight not to jump into his arms. Instead, she sat down at the nearest computer terminal and typed in the log-in and password Kotori gave her.

Fingers flying over the keys, she familiarized herself with Kotori's computer and then logged on to the Internet. She found the site that would give her remote access to her family's database and held her breath. The password was accepted, and she sighed in relief. Without a single qualm, she coded the system to delete eighty percent of the data. Afterward, she did a line-by-line search for anything they had on Alaska shifters and trashed it.

When her feet began to bother her, she winced and leaned away from the computer. She didn't have a chance to complain before Birk had dropped to his knees and begun removing her boots. Kotori, who had disappeared from the cabin, came in carrying a basin. The steam rising from it told her the water it held was hot. Kotori stooped beside Birk and placed the basin on the floor. He spun her chair so her feet were within his reach, and gently, he began to wash her feet with a warm, wet cloth.

Shiya leaned back in her chair and closed her eyes. A few moments later, something nudged her arm, and she looked up to find Birk had brought her cocoa. "I can't believe you two. Thank you."

She took the mug and sipped the hot liquid. Warmth stole over her body. When Kotori brought the temperature of her feet to a safe level, he placed them to soak in the water, and she couldn't help the moan that escaped her lips.

"If you do that, baby . . ." Birk began. Kotori only answered her moan with one of his own.

She grinned at them. "Just a little more. I have to tie up loose ends and send my family a message. I know how to cover myself so they can't trace it, so you don't have to worry about that." Neither man appeared to get what she was talking about, and didn't care. She laughed and moved the cordless keyboard to her lap to finish up her work. She would miss working for them, but she could no longer do it in good conscience. She had no intention of allowing them to kill shifters, so she attacked the backup systems, all that she'd set up herself.

With a few more taps, she sent off the message, including personal correspondence to Shae.

I'm sorry, sis, but this is what I feel I have to do. I'm not coming back. You were right. I love Birk and Kotori, and as long as they want me with them, this is where I will be. You know, as a Keith, I will protect my own. I will stand in the family's way of ever hurting them. Convince them, please, Shae. Convince them to pull out of Alaska and to never return. Know that I love you and Sakura and Dad. I even love that fool Kasen. This is my life to choose. Good-bye.

She double-checked her entry points and covered her tracks. Then she logged out of the system and off of the computer. When she put the keyboard up and turned to Birk and Kotori, she took them in—their handsome faces, their sexy builds, and most of all their gentle care of her.

She'd thought she loved Joe at one point, and when this first began, maybe she still did, but not now. Not when she felt consumed by the emotions she had for these two men.

Yeah, they were men. Real men who loved her and wanted to be with her. She sensed it and saw it in everything they did. Nothing came before her. Kotori had even called in his family to help save her. He'd exposed the existence of the other shifters on her behalf. She would never forget that or walk away knowing what he gave up for her.

Birk grabbed the towel that Kotori had brought in slung over his arm, and he used it to dry her feet before helping her to stand. They faced her, and she entwined her fingers with theirs, one hand joined with each. They leaned down and nuzzled her cheeks, their lips soft as they kissed their way to her throat. She trembled with pleasure, but moved back a little so she could speak. They watched her, interest in their gazes, paired with hunger. She wouldn't deny them for much longer.

"I love you two so much. I never thought I could feel this way. Definitely not for two men at the same time, and yet, it feels right."

Birk squeezed the hand he still held. "I love you, Shiya. You are my mate, and I was willing to give you up because I thought it was best for you. When you chose to stay with us, I couldn't deny myself again. I admit it. I'm selfish. I want you. So you better be ready for us."

"Oh, I'm ready." She raised an eyebrow and grinned.

Kotori grunted. "That's enough talking. I want you in my bed."

"Yes, sir!" The playful salute went wrong when Kotori's last bit of patience snapped, and he lifted her and thumped her down on the only bare spot of the desk and tore her jacket open. She looked down at the zipper bent beyond repair. "Well that's ruined."

Kotori followed by shoving her blouse and sweater up and ripping her bra to shreds. Her breasts filled his palms, and he bent his head to lick the pebbled nipples. Shiya moaned in ecstasy. She tangled her fingers in his hair and brought his head closer as she arched into his touch. When he reached between them to unbutton her pants and thrust a hand into the waistband, she didn't stop him. White-hot pleasure radiated her entire body when his fingers sank into her wet pussy. She humped his hand, wanting more. Even while she was exhausted, she needed to feel him inside of her.

"Kotori, fuck me now," she begged.

He sat up and ripped her pants down her legs and tore her panties to strips of cloth. His roughness only served to make her hotter, and she raised and spread her legs in invitation. Kotori stared down at her wetness, his eyes glazed over with lust. The button on his jeans hit the floor, and he scarcely got his pants and boxers down over his hips before he thrust into her.

Shiya screamed his name. He yanked her forward and pounded so deep, a shudder shook her from head to foot. Kotori drove into her, withdrew his dick, and then pounded in again. She hung on to his shoulders, head back and eyes closed. He ravaged her body, his pelvis brushing her sensitive clit until she had to grit her teeth to take it. An orgasm began to build, and she encouraged it, arching into her lover. The climax took hold. She found Kotori's mouth and kissed him. Their tongues curled together, Shiya moaning and tasting. She caught his bottom lip between her teeth, and he growled. He wrapped both arms around her and crushed her to his chest.

One final thrust, and his hot seed exploded into her channel.

Birk strode around the desk, and Kotori backed off. She thought her other lover would take her, but Birk hooked a finger in the air. "Get down."

She slid off of the desk and pulled her clothes on. She frowned, wondering what he was up to. She knew he wanted her—the tent in his pants a good indicator—but Birk led her from the cabin and along a row of others like it.

They headed toward the back of the compound, to a cabin set farther away from the others. All of a sudden, she knew Birk just wanted her somewhere more comfortable for the three of them.

The cabin was warm with a fire going in the fireplace. She noted it was smaller than the one they'd shared alone. A thick carpet covered the floor, and heavy, durable furniture decorated the place. At least here the curtains at the windows were nicer, and she guessed with women in the area, they had something to do with it. One bedroom was set off from the main area.

"Do you share this cabin?" she asked.

"It's mine," Kotori told her. "Birk lives closer to Juneau."

"But I'll be staying out here with you two, or at our other cabin, until I know the hunters have left the area." He strolled over to Shiya and turned her toward the bedroom. "You will be getting some rest after the long trek over here and your ordeal before that."

"But . . ."

"No buts." He swatted her ass. Shiya glanced up at him when he pushed her down onto the bed. Birk still had a hard-on, which she could take care of, but he refused until she got some sleep. Her heart swelled with love for him. She gave in to his encouragement to get some rest, and as soon as her head hit the pillow, she was out.

Shiya opened her eyes to a quiet room. No sounds reached her from the other room. She checked the clock on the bedside table and found she'd been out several hours. A long stretch pulled the kinks from her muscles, and she rose to go into the bathroom. A hot shower restored more of her energy, and she lingered in there, scrubbing strawberry-scented shower gel over her skin. Since she didn't imagine Kotori used the stuff, she figured Birk had borrowed it for her from one of the women. She silently thanked him and then rinsed off and stepped from the shower. She wondered where her lovers had gone. She missed them and wanted to spend every moment in their presence—at least for a while, until they got used to each other and the sense of being pulled apart passed.

She found lotion on the sink, the same brand and scent as the gel. Since it didn't appear to be a cheap kind, she smoothed some on her legs, over her belly and breasts, and down her arms. She grinned thinking how much Kotori would want to lick her when he got a whiff.

Shiya left the bathroom and froze. "What the hell?" Her eyes widened, and she took in the sight before her in unbelief. She glanced up toward the ceiling. "When did you . . . What do you plan to do with . . ."

The ropes she'd seen in Kotori and Birk's backpack at the other cabin now hung from the ceiling, and both her men were dressed in all black as if they waited to take her hostage in the most sensual of ways. Birk, in black fingerless gloves, manipulated the rope and offered her a suggestive smile.

"Kotori already had the hook, something he used for exercise equipment, he tells me. I suggested it would come in handy for playing with you."

She strolled closer to them and licked her lips at the image the two of them presented. Kotori, with his dark hair and eyes, along with his slightly darker skin than Birk's, set off the tight black cargo pants and long-sleeved black shirt to perfection. He'd even paired the outfit with black combat boots.

Where Birk's hands were covered in gloves, Kotori's big palms were bare.

Birk bent to reach into his pants pocket at the side of his thigh and pulled a ridged knife from its sheath. He twisted the rope into several knots and then hacked off the excess to let it fall to the floor. The sheer essence of danger had her heart pounding in her chest.

"This is for your body, honey, not your wrists." Birk frowned at the bruises still visible, and Kotori clenched his hands into fists. At the angry growl in his throat, she dropped her towel to the floor and moved closer to him. She watched the anger drain away as his desire grew.

"I'm all yours. Do whatever you want to me." She dropped her tone to something low and sultry, and both men looked like they were ready to eat her alive. Birk worked at a feverish pace to finish tying the rope the way he wanted, and then he looped it around her waist and across her breasts. The rope binding her breasts above and beneath seemed to accentuate them, and Kotori ran a thumb over first one nipple and then the other. She moaned and leaned into him, but Birk tugged her back.

"You stand there, and don't you move until I tell you to."

"Yes, sir."

He moved up behind her and ran a strip of the rope between her legs. By that time, she was so wet, she knew they must smell it. Kotori in front of her and Birk behind, her head swam with the possibilities.

She reached up on her toes to nip Birk's ear, but he moved away, a raised eyebrow in rebuke. She laughed, and he smacked her ass.

"Are you going to leave that between my legs?" she asked. "It will be hard to get inside me."

Birk pushed the rope against her opening. She caught her breath.

"You be quiet unless I give you permission to speak."

She pouted, and he leaned down to push his tongue between her lips. She took his kiss and offered herself to him. Birk squeezed her breast, pinched her nipple, and spanked her again. She craved more, but did her best to stay silent. She liked when he commanded her.

By the time Birk finished securing her, she couldn't move from the spot just beneath the hook on the ceiling, even if she wanted to. He ran a hand around in front of her and across her chest. When he raised her chin and turned her head, he covered her mouth with his. Birk didn't give her the chance to let him stick his tongue between her lips. He thrust in and swept the interior. She met the tip of his tongue with hers, trembling with desire.

Birk walked around in front of her, and Kotori stepped back. "Now, I want you to open my pants and free my cock."

Shiya did as she was told. Birk secured her in such a way that just her lower arms could move, with restriction, to obey him. The zipper was the only sound in the room other than her panting. Both Birk and Kotori seemed to be in calm control, while she felt like she needed to come, or she'd lose her mind. She had never imagined being at a man's mercy in this way could get her so hot.

She reached inside his pants and stroked his long, stiff cock. Precome coated the head, and she ran her thumb in it, wishing she could get a taste. Birk, reading her mind, swiped his cock head with a finger and pushed his finger between her lips. She sucked and moaned. Kotori groaned and stepped around Birk. He ran his fingers over the rope, allowing them to fall against her skin at each gap. He lingered at the swell of her breasts and played between them.

When he moved behind her and pushed a hand between her ass cheeks, she stuck her butt out toward him. He massaged her anus, and she murmured, "Yes, yes."

Birk jerked her forward, her bare feet skimming the floor. He spanked her hard enough on the ass to cause a sting. Her pussy clenched, and she knew she grew wetter.

"I'm sorry," she moaned.

Another swat, and she closed her eyes, clamping her teeth together. Kotori added to her punishment when he pinched both her nipples until they ached. She couldn't help it. She cried out in pleasure. This time, Birk didn't spank her. He parted her legs and thrust two fingers into her pussy. He pumped hard and fast so that his palm smacked against her clit. Shiya tried to hold off, but she lost control. Sensations overwhelmed her. Her core muscles contracted, sending rays of bliss throughout every inch of her body. Before her orgasm could take full effect, Birk withdrew his hand and yanked his pants down. His cock stretched her pussy, filling it.

Deeper, deeper! Please!

Birk held on to the rope at her hips and ground into her pussy. Because of the way he'd bound her, she couldn't get a firm grip on the floor. He'd hoisted her just an inch or so beyond where her toes reached, and he didn't allow her to raise her legs to wrap around his waist. That made his entrance into her channel tighter than normal. She loved every single thrust.

Shiya put a hand down between them to feel Birk's cock sliding into her. Her fingertips skimmed over his rod, and a moan escaped her. She wished she could rotate her hips and give as much as she got, but Birk kept her still. He pounded into her until she thought she'd lose her mind. Then he stopped.

Her head fell forward, and she mourned the loss of the full feeling. *Don't stop.*

Kotori took Birk's place. He unbuttoned his pants himself and freed his cock. One sharp push, and he crammed his dick into her pussy.

"Kotori!" She clutched at his shirt as high as she could raise her arms. Like Birk, he held on to her hips and ground into her. He took his thrusts slower, waiting for her pussy to stretch a little more. She knew it was a matter of time before he lost it.

"Damn this rope," Kotori growled. "I want you to be a part of me, as one."

She understood what he meant. Kotori loved crushing her full length to him, enveloping her in every sense. The rope stood somewhat as a barrier, and yet it seemed to drive him wilder, made him hungrier to claim her body. His thrusts picked up speed, the friction between them electric. Kotori shifted his hands to her ass and drove her into his cock. She raised her legs a bit more to accommodate him.

"I'm going to come too soon!" Kotori pulled out, and Birk slipped back inside her. Kotori moved behind, and for the first time, it occurred to Shiya that they hadn't used protection since the beginning. Could she have their baby? Did she want to?

Birk snapped her chin up. "Is your mind wandering? We must be boring you."

"Can't let that happen." Kotori rifled through items out of her sight, and then she felt the smooth creaminess of lubricant being smeared on her ass. She almost whooped with excitement.

This time Birk raised her legs all the way so that they wound around his waist. He didn't slow his amazing thrusts for a second, and he captured her lips with his for a long, hungry kiss. Shiya forgot everything she was thinking while she sucked her lover's tongue, and then Kotori eased his big cock into her ass. Her forehead dropped onto Birk's shoulder, and she shut her eyes.

Birk slowed to a stop and waited while Kotori worked deeper and deeper. The squeeze felt impossible, but she loved it.

"Yes, fill me up! It's so tight. Yes, Kotori. Birk!"

They both pushed in at the same time, all the way to the hilt. She cried out their names once again. All energy left her body, but when her two lovers began to move, she lost it. Her orgasm crashed through her center, and all reasonable thought left. She writhed the best she could, encouraging every repeating ripple of sensation. Birk pumped harder, and so did Kotori. They grunted and groaned, shouting their pleasure. When she came to the end of her rope mentally, Birk stopped moving and came. She felt his scorching come warm her insides. He pumped into her once and then again, finishing it. When he was done, he held her still against Kotori while he wore her poor ass out. Kotori came at last, and his come filled her hole and dripped out to the tops of her thighs. He collapsed on her shoulder, and the three of them stood there, unmoving.

When Shiya's breathing returned to normal, Birk pulled his knife from its casing once again. He cut her free of the rope and carried her to the bed. One man lay on one side of her, while the second occupied the other. Shiya absorbed the love she sensed as they touched her, and she settled against

Birk's chest. Kotori scooted up close behind, and she took his hand to lay it over her breast. He spooned her ass, sending shock waves through her in memory of the pleasure and pain he'd given her moments ago.

"Hey," Birk whispered.

She'd closed her eyes and didn't bother opening them again. A yawn forced her to move just to cover her mouth, but then she settled in. "Hm?"

"Being with us won't be easy for you, Shiya. Do you understand that?"

"Yes."

"Do you?" Kotori insisted.

She sighed. "The way I see it, I don't have a choice. Seriously, I can't imagine being with anyone other than the two of you. I can't bear the thought of going away and leaving you. So, hard or not, I'm in it for the long haul. If you two are too weak to handle me . . ."

Kotori grunted, and Shiya laughed.

"I think we're pretty much decided," Birk said.

She put a hand on her bare hip. "Excuse me? Pretty much?"

He raised his hands and shrugged as if he didn't know for sure.

"Oh no you didn't." She sat up, all tiredness gone. "I see I'm going to have to show you a little something so you know just who it is you are having sex with."

Shiya shoved Birk onto his back and straddled his hips. The moment she brought her pussy down, his cock went rock hard. She reached under her and guided it inside. Birk groaned his pleasure. He seemed to struggle not to let things go too far yet, his fingers digging into her hips to keep her still.

"Are you sure, Shiya?" he asked.

She ignored him and raised her legs. After licking her middle finger, she pressed the tip to her clit and rotated it a circle. With her other hand, she played with her nipple, all the while making sexy sounds she knew would get them worked up. Kotori sat up, his dark eyes riveted on her movements. Birk lost the grip he had on her hips, and she began to grind on his cock.

"You naughty, naughty woman," Birk moaned, raising his hips to thrust into her.

Kotori took his shaft into his hands and began stroking while he watched. "I want some of that."

"You're next," she told him. "I'm not stopping until my men are good and satisfied. Then you will be convinced that I'm exactly what you've been looking for."

"Yes, ma'am," they echoed together, and the matter was soon settled.

"So, what are we going to do, Daddy?" Shae folded her arms over her chest. A deep fear for her sister's safety tightened the muscles in her stomach. She felt like screaming and telling the man what she wanted done, but things didn't work like that with her father. No one crossed him, and if she even dared, she'd find herself on a flight back to San Diego, cut off from the family business. That wasn't happening. She wanted a part of every asshole who had the bad luck of being born a beast, and now that two of them had brainwashed her sister, she really wanted them all dead.

Her father pinched the bridge of his nose and paced Shiya's suite. "She's crippled us, Shae. Most of our information is gone. We're back to square one. I put too much faith in Shiya handling that side of things."

"Let's go get those bastards that have her."

His expression hardened. "No, we pull out of Alaska."

"What!"

He gave her a look, and she pressed her lips together.

He spun on his heel and shouted orders to the men milling around. Soon the entire operation was closed down, and they were on a flight back home. This was their first failure after her mother's death, and if it killed her, she vowed it would be the last.

About the Author

Tressie Lockwood has always loved books, and she enjoys writing about heroines who are overcoming the trials of life. She writes straight from her heart, reaching out to those who find it hard to be themselves completely no matter what anyone else thinks. She hopes her readers enjoy her short stories. Visit Tressie on the Web at www.tressielockwood.com.